Praise for Animus Paradox

"Cyberpunk-y mystery and mayhem I absolutely devoured!"
—**Andy Peloquin,** author of Cerberus.

"Fast-paced and adrenaline-pumping, this cyberpunk tale set in a futuristic and rich Italian city reads just like a movie. With heists and action galore, fans of Blade Runner and Mission Impossible won't be disappointed, and will likely forget that they are reading a book and not watching the high-stakes scenes play before them on a screen."
—**Nina Voss,** author of *Neon Noir.*

"[Animus Paradox] brings together [multiple] conflicts, John Wick style high velocity action, and futuristic world building into a gripping page turner."
—**Paul G. Zareith,** author of *Revenge of the Wraith Paladin* (SFF Insiders)

"This is a noir cyberpunk story to a T. You want robotics and blood, you got it!"
—**Bill Adams,** author of The Divine Godsqueen Coda, and *Unlucky Evens, Cursed Odds.* (FanFiAddict)

"[Animus Paradox has] lots of action from the start, the story moves quickly, even as the plot becomes more complex with each new twist in the investigation."
—**A.J. Calvin,** author of The Caein Legacy and The Relics of War series. (FanFiAddict)

"*Animus Paradox* is a tour de force of cyberpunk story-telling. Bassett expertly blends the high-tech setting, societal angst, and countercultural aspirations one would expect from the genre with a gritty, engrossing, and mysterious neo-noir private detective story. Beyond all the intriguing cybernetics, digital chicanery, and thrilling gunplay, the world is fleshed out with an amazing fusion of cultures that made me want to get lost there, and the characters have an emotional depth that will draw you in and have you on the edge of your seat rooting for them."
—**B.K. Bass,** author of The Night Trilogy and editor for *Animus Paradox.*

ANIMUS PARADOX.

BY **ADAM BASSETT**

eBook ISBN: 979-8-9909819-2-8
Paperback ISBN: 979-8-9909819-3-5

Cover Illustration by Ahmed Elgharabawy
Cover Design by Adam Bassett
Map & Interior Illustrations by Adam Bassett

First Edition 2025

Dedication

For my friend, B.K.

About Content Warnings

Animus Paradox is intended for mature audiences. It contains some descriptions and scenes that may be off-putting to some readers. If you would like to know more, please flip to the back of the book, where I've listed a few content warnings (as spoiler-free as possible).

Central Italy

North Lazio · 2167

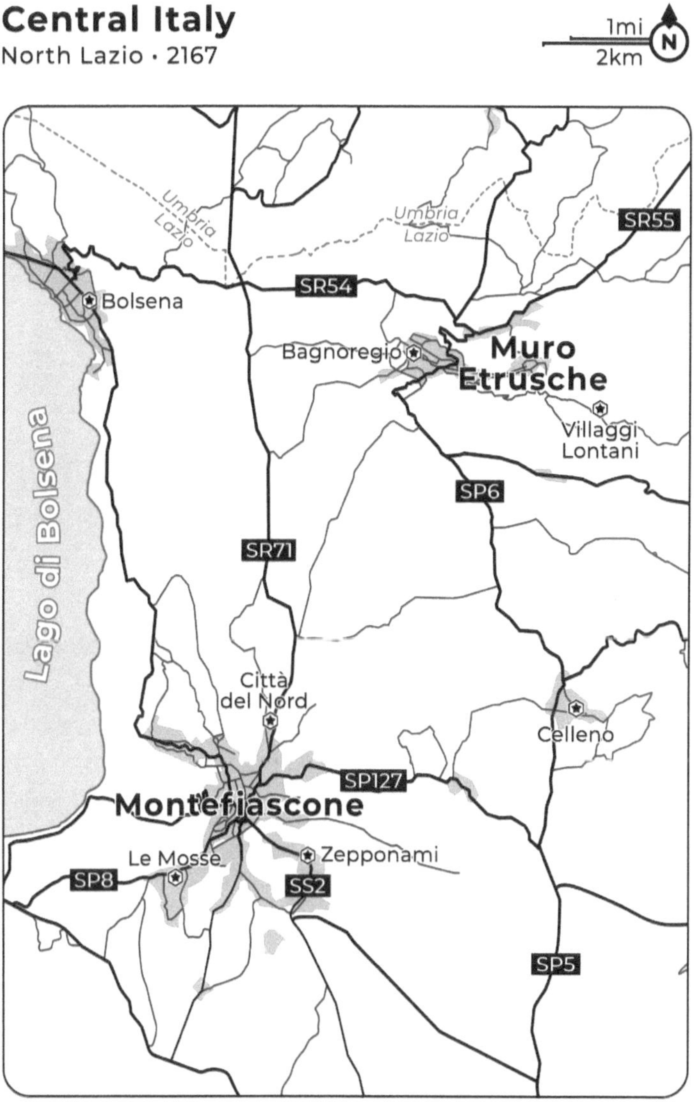

Chapter 01

Italy, 2167

IN THE EARLY HOURS of the new year, as fireworks' smoke still lingered in the midnight air, David wondered if he was still cut out to be a private investigator. Just minutes ago he had rescued the once-missing Segreti boy. The kid was in the back seat. Before they got in the car, Mafalda had found tarps to place underneath them both to keep the car clean. David and the boy had only just emerged from the innards of a muddy hill, excavated with Maf's help, and a friend from the police department.

The rescue had been a close one. Had David not acted on a hunch, the boy probably would have been trapped underground, without a way to signal for help. Had David not retained a few mods from his time in the U.S. military, he wouldn't have been able to get a message to his wife, and Maf wouldn't have known where to dig them out. A lot of things had to go right for them to have escaped the underground, most of which came down to luck. There was always a bit of that in his line of work—being at the right place at the right time—but just earlier that night he and the boy almost suffocated in mud and darkness.

Maf hadn't spoken much since the fireworks ended. She had both hands on the wheel, hair blowing in the wind, a soft yellow glow emanating from the folds of her jacket and a pair of kanji tattooed on her neck. Captions appeared on the lower third of his heads-up display in light blue translating the characters: *[Family]*.

If she was bothered by the fact he'd nearly been buried alive, Maf didn't show it in front of the kid. She was working through something, though. Her eyes were on the road, but her thoughts seemed miles away. David opened his mouth to say something to her, but he couldn't decide what, and looked out the window instead.

They were entering the neighborhood of Calanchi, where the dense skyscrapers and mixed-use development of Muro Etrusche became smaller apartments and offices, then single-family homes with hedges and backyard pools. Windows revealed dioramas of people's lives, each celebrating the new year. Some raised glasses to the sky, others crowded around a card table, a few more found each other below a sprig of mistletoe.

They arrived at the Segreti's home as snow began to fall. His parents hadn't seen the boy in several days. They sobbed and chided him in Italian. They spoke through tears and fumbled their words so badly that David's translator only caught pieces of the conversation. He knew enough of the language that the moment was not lost on him. David waited quietly in the doorway with Maf. She leaned against him and wrapped her fingers around his. Mud rubbed between their hands.

The Segretis paid the remainder of David's fee, plus a couple hundred euros extra. Perhaps they assumed he—an American—required a tip. Perhaps they were just grateful. Numbers flickered across his vision, adding to his checking account. As his balance disappeared, an automated message took its place:

[12:42] Transfer received from IT009-250. Thank you for choosing Uni-Intesa Bank!

David and Maf thanked the Segretis, and returned to the car. Maf reached for the key switch, but let her hand slip back onto her lap. The engine remained still. Snow began to collect on the windshield. Maf stared straight ahead through it at the idyllic neighborhood beyond. A chill hung in the air.

"I'm glad you found the boy, David, I truly am," she said. Even inside the car, her breath misted white in the air, illuminated by a yellow streetlight above them. "I just... I can't believe you went into those tunnels. If Quintino and I hadn't gotten to you in time…"

David nodded. They hadn't had a chance to speak about what happened yet, but she knew the gist. She'd been there when Quintino and his officers dug them out of the tunnels below Civita di Bagnoregio.

"I'm just so tired," she continued. "Lately, every job starts as 'my *whoever* is missing' and turns into—"

"'My *whoever* is making bombs,'" David finished.

"I was going to say 'is cheating on me with a member of the Tigres,' but the bomb maker was a fun one too," she said. A weak laugh escaped her lips. "Speaking of which, our Tigres friends messaged me a while ago. They will be back in the morning. We got a lead on the Hayasaka job."

"Hm." David frowned.

They had no Tigres *friends*—though they'd worked alongside plenty of them over the years. They were all over the city—embedded into the police, government, small businesses, anything they could get their hands on. They weren't all bad, but the Tigres pledged allegiance to their boss over anything else. That made them dangerous. Not to mention the way disaster seemed to follow them around. It seemed to David that the Tigres and their enemies seemed equally trigger-happy.

"I need your help with this case," Maf said.

"I would have given it the other night, when you told me the Tigres involved themselves, if I wasn't already on another case. Now that the boy's back home, I expect a full briefing."

Mafalda grinned at him, flicked the key switch, and the car hummed to life. His heads-up display blinked red at him, his optics' battery ticking down from fifteen percent, as Maf kissed his cheek. He didn't want to plug in. Not yet. But the clock was ticking.

Fourteen percent.

David put a hand on Maf's leg, his eyes lingering on her. She watched the road, a sliver of a smile on her lips. If he weren't so tired, David would have had her pull over in a dark corner of Calanchi. He had a sense that she was thinking about the same thing, though she must have been just as exhausted, as she kept on toward home.

The last few days had been nonstop, each of them chasing down their quarries. They'd be busy in the morning, but they would be working together this time. They always did their best work together. They'd make quick work of the Tigres' contract, and then they'd be on to the next job. Hopefully a less exciting one.

The windows rattled as a gust struck the apartment, and a flurry of snow was knocked off of the rooftop. The squall roused

David from his sleep. His optics flicked on, and the world came into view. His HUD informed him about the weather and battery levels. The latest headlines scrolled along the bottom of his vision—interspersed by ads for new Jeeps and discounted bikinis. He dismissed them with a thought, then disconnected the cable from the side of his head. The battery charge immediately ticked down to ninety-nine percent.

David's eyes had been replaced during his time with the military. The army had given him a handful of mods, most of which had been disabled after he left active duty, but the eyes remained. Metal and wire spidered out from around them, lacing together across the bridge of his nose and stretching toward his temples. The eyes themselves were black, a byproduct of their infrared and night vision capabilities. His irises, however, were a light blue—his favorite color. Although, sometimes he would turn them yellow—Maf's favorite.

His optics had been cutting-edge twenty years ago. These days, just about anyone could pick up a pair of oracles if they had the euros for them. David was grateful for that. People were finally getting used to seeing folk with mechanical eyes. Most didn't even bother to ask about them anymore. He just wished they held a charge for longer. He used to get thirty hours, but now he had to jack back in after just twenty. He only got half of that if he used night vision regularly.

Maf rested her head on his chest, her hair flowing over him like an onyx river. David ran a hand through it, tucking a strand behind her ear. As he did, she traced her finger along a seam in his right arm. The mechanical one. Just beneath the metal was a long blade, another gift courtesy of the U.S. army. Just in case somebody snuck up on him. It had protected him against assassins, thieves, and special ops. He'd even used it to slice apples, once. A trusty blade could do both, an officer once told him. David could still remember Lin's laugh, though he couldn't recall what she looked like without the aid of his external memory anymore. She'd been one of his few superiors close to his age. Lin must have been pushing sixty years old. Christ, David thought, *he* was getting old.

Before David and the Segreti boy escaped the tunnels, the child had noticed the seams in his arm and asked if David had ever used the blades underneath. He'd told the boy no, but he could still feel the weight of the hidden blade and the blood on his hands. He'd hoped once that when the army disabled his combat mods he'd become somebody new and put everything behind him. That hadn't quite happened. He'd spent a few too many years in the service, taking down security systems and watching divers' backs as they sat in ice baths and entered the Net. He'd become a living weapon—a tool to keep their divers alive by any means necessary. He'd been damn good at it, too.

"I'm going to get us some coffee," Maf announced, sitting up but not quite getting out of bed.

She leaned over the side and picked an old sweatshirt of David's off the floor and slipped it on—his old UNYU hoodie. There was a bullet hole near the second *U*, courtesy of an encounter with the Tigres. He'd stitched it up since then, and they were on good enough terms now, but David felt the scar on his chest itch whenever he saw the old tear.

"David," she said. Her smile was stunning. She ran a finger in circles on his chest. Her nail ran along a metal implant that helped to keep his dermal wrap together, a kind of exoskeleton. He barely noticed it anymore, and it had saved his life more than once. Hence the scratches and dents from myriad knives and bullets.

"Coffee?" Maf whispered.

David grunted and rolled out from underneath the covers. "No," he said, exaggerating each word. "Don't get up. I'll get us coffee."

"Thank you," Maf grinned at him in mock surprise, clearly enjoying her victory.

David dimmed his optics' brightness as he stepped into the kitchen. He picked the Vietnamese robusta—Maf's favorite. The beans were a bit strong for his taste, but David could fix that with a little extra milk and creamer.

While the coffee brewed, he grabbed a bottle of wine from the fridge and took a swig from it, a fruity Prosecco from Valdobbiadene. It was left over from the other night when he helped Maf sift through a pile of trash they'd found at an abandoned Rivoluzionari hideout. They'd found a load of discarded chrome there: body mods like his and components for them. It alluded to the hideout having been used as a blood clinic—an unregistered and unregulated place for mod installations. Sometimes the owner had just fallen on hard times, but usually those clinics were just operating around the law, installing parts not yet approved for public use. At worst, they were giving military-grade gear to whoever could afford it.

The fact the abandoned spot was a hole in the wall at the end of a dark alley, tucked away from any cameras, suggested the worst.

Among the pile of junk they'd brought back, Maf had found a logo, and he'd confirmed it the morning before with his enhanced vision. It belonged to a proper clinic operating in Zepponami, a town just south of the city. Last he knew, Maf and the Tigres had gone to take a look at the place.

David put the wine away and gave the pile of rubbish still on their kitchen table a quick scan. The gear was all a few years out of date, some dating back as far as the turn of the twenty-second century: pieces of dermal wraps, data shards, and a few whole limbs. Half a dozen had the same *Zepponami* logo. They were all faded and scratched, deliberately defaced.

The coffee maker beeped at him angrily, a green light flashing on the side of it.

When David returned to the bedroom, Maf had changed into a white shirt, dark blue jeans, and her favorite pleather jacket. She pulled her hair back into a bun as he set her coffee down on the dresser.

"Client messaged you?" David asked.

She nodded. "The Tigres got us access to that clinic in Zepponami. We found it yesterday—"

"The one that you had me I.D."

"[Yes,]" she said in Italian. Then, in English, "But when we arrived, it was crawling with police. They weren't pleased to see us, and stopped me from looking around. But Gennoveffa says that the Tigres worked it out, got us access."

David took a sip of his coffee. "Glad Mama Cinzia's on our side. For now, at least."

Maf grinned, putting on a pair of small hoop earrings. "You just be glad Mama's in charge of them now. The Tigres' last leader was a butcher."

"What was his name, Papa Macabre?"

"No, just [The Butcher.] Although some people called him Frankenstein on account of his mods—he had an old model of external memory that kind of made it look like he had bolts sticking out each side of his head. If you looked at it from the right angle, at least."

David laughed. "Well, I'm going to take a shower, then."

"I'll catch you up on everything with the job once you're out."

"Or... You could join me."

She raised an eyebrow at him.

"To save time," David muttered over the rim of his mug.

"Oh, [love,] you're about ten minutes too late."

"I knew I should have made instant coffee, but I just had to pick *your* favorite."

"Oh you did? *Thank you.*" She picked the mug up and took a long drink. "Oh, that's good. Now stop whining. I'll join you next time," Maf added with a wink.

Chapter 02

DAVID FIXED HIS TIE while Maf explained the situation to him. Hayasaka Hachirō stole money from Mama Cinzia—that was how the Tigres got involved—and then he went missing. He previously had an apartment in Kanagawa. Maf had looked into it, but that part of the city had flooded years ago, and there was no sign as of yet that he'd returned to Japan, anyway. As for his apartment in Muro Etrusche, Maf had already checked that as well and found it was empty. She hid a camera by the front door but it hadn't picked up on anyone going in or out since. His sister had come by and knocked a few times, but she didn't have a key or any info on where he might have gone. She'd been the one to kick off the job before the Tigres forced themselves into it.

Hachirō was a medical engineer who transitioned into clinic work installing mods. Maf suspected that he'd been the one to remove the chrome that sat in their kitchen, though they had no official record of it. If there were any, she suggested that the records were in Zepponami, but it was more likely that none were ever filed in the first place.

The clinic was under new ownership, but there'd been a shooting a few days ago and it was still on lockdown while police investigators looked into the situation. That meant whatever deal the Tigres had worked out with Zepponami's police department, they would probably have the place to themselves for the most part.

Aside from all of that, there was a chance that Hachirō was working with the Rivoluzionari, a group of rebels that had been making problems for the Italian government for almost a decade. That seemed likely, since they found the chrome in a Rivoluzionari hideout, but it was impossible to confirm yet. Even if he was working with them, to what degree? Was he helping to fund their operation, or were they just his source for black market parts? Would they interfere and fight for him when David and Maf showed up with the Tigres, or throw the surgeon under the bus?

David fastened his holster to his belt. It contained a Beretta M2161-V, a simple black service weapon similar to the kind he used in the military. It wasn't anything flashy; it didn't use any railtech to make the bullets go faster, or anything of the sort. It was just a simple firearm with a low risk of jamming. The kind of tool that got the job done. He hoped he wouldn't need it, but better safe than sorry. Besides, while she spoke, Maf had already grabbed hers. It was tucked away in a shoulder holster, concealed under her jacket.

"So, we're going to Zeppo," Maf finished. "The police there shouldn't give us any trouble. Gennoveffa says that's taken care of. Sounds like a one-time deal, though. We'll go in, have a look around, and hopefully that will lead us closer to Hachirō."

"One-time deal," David repeated. "If there's no lead, is there a plan B?"

"Sure isn't."

David blinked at her.

"Don't look at me like that, I don't have a lot to go on. Come on, finish your coffee, the Tigres will be here in five."

The Tigres arrived exactly five minutes later, at 9:53 AM. David had already met them a few days ago, briefly, when Maf asked him to help look around the old Rivoluzionari hideout. He reintroduced himself anyway.

Gennoveffa was at the wheel. Her hair was long, tied back in a braid that reached the small of her back. Her right arm was more metal than flesh, and a mod cradled the side of her head such that her hair was shaved along one side. The mod itself seemed to be some kind of retrofitted module for working in the Net—or perhaps a space between the Net and the Real. Interfacing with cameras and data shards more quickly, sending remote signals—a more limited version of what David used to be able to do.

While Gennoveffa was outfitted with tools that seemed to help her work between worlds, Jun'ichi was a classic bruiser. His hair was slicked back, and an array of steel around his orange-ringed eyes stretched back behind one ear. His eyes weren't synthetic, but they were as close as a person could get—outfitted with advanced lenses combined with a sleek-looking external memory. A dermal wrap stretched around most of his body, with seams along his legs that suggested something else hidden underneath. It closely resembled David's military model, though a few parts on his shoulders and neck had even thicker plating. It was the kind that could stop a few bullets, provided they didn't hit the same spot too many times.

Both carried pistols on their hips, and a sheathed katana rested next to Jun'ichi. The grip was wrapped in black cotton in a diamond pattern revealing the cream-colored surface beneath it. The Tigres also bore identical light tattoos: glowing orange tigers baring long fangs that resembled bullets.

"David's going to help us out," Maf told them as she climbed into the back seat of their car.

The two looked at one another. "[I will need to tell Mama Cinzia about this,]" Gennoveffa said in Italian.

"I won't get in the way," David said, following Maf into the car. "My last case just finished, and I want to lend a helping hand now that I can." It was mostly true. He did want to help, especially considering he didn't fully trust anyone who bore the Tigre brand.

"[Mama Cinzia does not like surprises,]" Gennoveffa said. Then, in heavily accented English, "That right, Jun?"

Jun'ichi nodded.

"[It will just be a second.]" Gennoveffa stared into the distance, her eyes glittering red as she messaged Mama Cinzia, or more likely one of her assistants. David doubted that the enforcer had a direct line to her boss. The lights flickered and disappeared from her eyes, and she refocused on David. "[You may join, but the Tigres will not pay more for your services than what has already been agreed to.]"

"I didn't expect it," David said. "You're already paying the investagatori privati—that's both Maf and I."

Gennoveffa smiled at him, revealing sharpened canines. "[Why didn't you just say you'd work for free?]" she said and spun to face the wheel.

Traffic was slow in the city, where manned and automated vehicles alike fought for space. The streets were wide, but there were so many intersections—so many points at which they could be stopped. That changed abruptly as Gennoveffa steered onto SP6, abandoning the city for the rolling hills surrounding it.

It took about half an hour to reach Zepponami, a small town centered around a stretch of SS2. In recent years, it had become a kind of suburb of Montefiascone, just as dense as the city at its center. Small shops like *Macelleria Rossi* and *Self Service Tabacchi* clung to the old sidewalks, their beige concrete walls transitioning to brutalist steel apartments above. Wherever one collapsed, it was replaced by a modern office or hotel, the glassy façade reflecting the town back at itself, flickering neon signs even under the morning sun.

The Zepponami clinic was located on a dirt road that led away from Via Giranesi. It threaded through several old neighborhoods. The clinic itself was nestled into the center of a small shopping center attached to a few warehouses. Its sign bore the same *Zepponami Clinic* logo that David and Maf found on the discarded chrome, and an unlit neon window sign that read *[body improvements]* in Japanese.

A state police officer stepped forward as they got out of the car.

"[Stand down,]" Gennoveffa told him as she walked toward the door. There was no hesitation in her voice or stride. "[We have an invite, courtesy of Mama Cinzia. I'm sure you heard.]"

The man hesitated, then stepped aside. "[You have fifteen minutes.]"

Gennoveffa stopped and glanced back at Maf. "[Is fifteen enough?]"

"[I'd prefer more, but I'll see what I can do,]" she said.

"We'll split up," David added. "I can help cover more ground."

Gennoveffa looked poised to argue, but must have decided against it, and followed them to the clinic's front entrance.

Inside, the lobby led to a window where—presumably—an office worker would have taken patients' information. David could see an office through the window. Around the corner were a few empty chairs, a faux potted plant, and an empty water cooler. The jug had been drained completely, and some of the paper cups had toppled onto the floor.

"Let's have a look around, then," David said, pushing through the door that led deeper into the clinic.

It led to a long hallway with several surgical rooms leading away from it. One end appeared to lead toward the office, and the other went to a small storage room. Maf went toward the office, so David walked in the opposite direction. Gennoveffa followed him into the garage, looming over his shoulder as he picked through boxes of mods, parts, and medical supplies. Some of it had been cleared away already, possibly for the police's investigation, but most remained.

David wasn't quite sure what he was looking for, but if the clinic had been conducting some illicit deals or peddling illegal mods, there might be some evidence of that tucked away here. He would have gone through all of it manually, but the police's clock was ticking. He guessed that they only had thirteen minutes left. David gave the whole room a scan with his optics, and a list of parts appeared in the corner of his vision. He scrolled through them, looking for a bright red icon that would mark anything as banned for civilian use. A few items came up, but they were mostly in the form of outdated parts. That could spell trouble for the owners, but it didn't point toward Hachirō or the Rivoluzionari. Just corporate mismanagement.

David adjusted his scan's parameters and ran it again. This time, something odd caught his attention. Behind the garage door, somebody was listening to them. He picked them up by a few signals their mods were giving off, probably a cochlear implant and possibly biocompressors. It could have been somebody from the police, but he could pick up signals from their mods as well. They hadn't moved from where they'd greeted him, Maf, and the Tigres.

David caught Gennoveffa's eye. It took a few seconds, as she was preoccupied with a box of old data shards—most of which appeared to be burnt or cracked. He pointed toward his cochlear implant, and he sent her his contact information.

A moment passed before she messaged him, her text instantly translated into English as it arrived on his HUD: *[10:02] What?*

David pointed toward a side entrance in the garage and replied: *[10:02] Somebody's out there.*

She wrinkled her brow at him, then nodded. *[10:02] Your eyes pick something up?*

David nodded.

[10:02] Are they armed? she asked.

[10:03] I'm not sure, but I am pretty sure they're not police. Would anyone else be sneaking around here?

Gennoveffa drew her pistol.

[10:03] Get Mafalda and Jun'ichi. We may need to leave quickly.

David hurried back to the office. Maf was on the computer, lights flickering across her eyes as she reviewed and downloaded the clinic's files. Her hard wire was jacked into the old desktop, the cable emerging from her wrist. Jun'ichi leaned against a wall, quietly watching the police through the window.

"Somebody's sneaking around the garage," David whispered.

Jun'ichi stood up and walked out without a word.

"Okay, I guess. I think we might be out of time, Maf. Do you have what you need?" David asked.

"I don't know. At this point, I'm just grabbing whatever I can, taking pictures with my lenses," she said, gesturing toward the contact lenses on her eyes. "Who would—"

Gunshots rang out from the garage. Maf pulled her hard wire from the computer and it snapped back into her wrist. David took her hand and pulled her to her feet. They sprinted out of the office, and through the waiting room. As they exited the clinic, Jun'ichi was starting the car, and the police were shouting at them. David couldn't see what was shooting at them, or perhaps who the Tigres had shot at. He and Maf reached the car just as Gennoveffa did. She shouted at Jun'ichi, "[Follow the red Fiat!]"

Jun'ichi pressed the accelerator to the floor and the tires squealed. The Fiat raced ahead of them, its motor buzzing, dodging cars and scooters down the narrow streets of Zeppon- ami. David tried to scan the car, but they were too far away, and Jun'ichi's driving was making it hard to concentrate. He sped after it, drifting around a bend like he was auditioning for Hollywood. David felt his body pulled to the side, then fell back against his seat as Jun'ichi straightened out and sped up. David clipped on his seat belt.

"[Who is it?]" Maf shouted.

"[Looked like a member of Heredes,]" Gennoveffa said.

David felt his stomach turn. Working with the Tigres was frustrating, but they could be dealt with. Mama Cinzia and her enforcers found reason in euros and services. The Heredes were zealots—they either got what they wanted, or they *took* it. They'd been gone for years, though. Why would they have come back?

To Jun'ichi, Gennoveffa said, "[Pull up alongside her, I'll shoot out her tires.]"

Jun'ichi grunted at her and tilted his head at the traffic. There was no room to weave through it—but that also meant that the Fiat was having trouble getting too far away from them. Jun'ichi had brought them about thirty meters apart, and that was likely all he'd be able to do while in town. And they were headed north, toward Montefiascone, where traffic would only worsen. They needed to act, or the Heredes would get away.

"Do either of you have a remote installed?" David asked.

His was disabled after leaving the army, but the Tigres were known to have some quality blood clinicians—surgeons who installed mods under the counter. It was a well-known fact that many Tigres were using military-grade mods, but the police often had trouble tracking them down or were outmaneuvered.

Jun'ichi glanced back at him, then turned back to the road, banking left. Another car had somehow gotten between them and the Fiat.

David pressed on. "Look, we're working together. If I turn you in, my ass is probably cooked too. And you both know Mama Cinzie would help you. So, do you have a remote, or even a quick-breach module?"

An arm reached out of the Fiat's window, pistol in hand, and fired off a few shots. A hole erupted in the windshield, shards of glass dangling from the wound.

People on the sidewalk shouted and scrambled inside the nearest building. David heard sirens in the distance.

"I have a QBM," Gennoveffa said.

"Great. Don't worry about the driver or engine, their chrome will be too resistant to you anyway. But you should be able to trigger the car's brakes from here. Find them, but don't activate them yet."

"You think you can force them to turn off the main road?" Maf asked.

"Exactly," David said. "Gotta' get us off these streets. If you can trigger her brakes on the right side of the vehicle as she's approaching a turn, the car will naturally swing to the right. Just before this road here. With some luck—"

The Fiat skidded suddenly and spun toward the right. It wavered, then veered down Via Grilli, a narrow but mostly empty road that led away from Zepponami.

"Perfect," David said, nearly biting his tongue as Jun'ichi rounded the same corner.

The Fiat regained control over its brakes. Whether that was because Gennoveffa let her hold over them go or the driver wrested control back, David couldn't tell. It raced past the abandoned dump, traveling down the middle of the road to prevent them from overtaking it. The car kicked up slush and mud as the pavement ended, making both of their cars skid and swerve. Gennoveffa aimed out her window and took a few shots. Her pistol gave off an electric hum, then she squeezed the trigger, and shots echoed against the buildings. David spotted a few new bullet holes above the Fiat's left rear wheel as it moved to the left side of the road. She'd almost gotten it.

Jun'ichi was already accelerating up the right lane. Gennoveffa grabbed the wheel and he let go all at once, drawing his own pistol, and put two bullets into one of the Fiat's wheels. The red car spun out and crashed into a fence, skidding between a few large beech trees and into the old dump. As Jun'ichi spun their car around, David heard the Fiat slam into the twenty-first century detritus.

"You two stay in the car," Gennoveffa told David and Maf as they steered toward the break in the fence. "They might be armed."

"Try not to kill them," Maf said. "[We can't always get answers from a corpse.]"

Gennoveffa gave Maf a long stare. As Jun'ichi brought the car to a stop, she left without a word.

The Fiat had crashed into a pile of trash on the edge of the old dump. Its left side was scratched up badly, silver scars where paint used to be, and the grill was badly dented by a large dumpster. David could see the driver moving around inside, but they hadn't left the vehicle yet.

Jun'ichi retrieved his sword from the car and pulled it from the sheath, revealing the blade, shimmering in the late-morning sunlight. He took a stance outside the Fiat's driver door. Gennoveffa approached along the passenger side.

"They're going to kill her," Maf told David.

He grunted in response.

Outside, the Tigres approached the Fiat.

Gennoveffa shouted, "[Step out of the car, slowly, and keep your hands up!]"

The driver was still moving about in their car, but the door remained closed.

"[This is your final warning!]"

David took another scan of the Fiat. From there, he could see a bit better. Inside, a woman was giving him drastically different readings than she had outside of the garage. Her bio-compressors were using an abnormally high amount of energy. An unsustainable amount, in fact. Then, the signal from her cochlear implant was cut off.

"Something's not right," he told Maf. "It's like she's over-loading her mods. They shouldn't be under that much stress. Why—"

The Fiat's door erupted off its hinges, and the driver leapt out, rolling on the ground. Snow clung to her hair and clothes. Light tattoos glowed a bright blue, snaking up her arms and culminating in a crown tattooed into each of her forearms: the mark of the Heredes.

As the woman recovered from the leap, she brought a handgun up and fired a few shots. A few slammed into their car. David heard Maf shout. The Heredes woman moved to sprint, but Jun'ichi was already at her side. A lightning-quick arc of his blade and the woman's right hand—still clutching the handgun—fell on the snow. Crimson blossomed around it. She screamed and ran at Jun'ichi. Seams parted in her left arm, and a hidden blade emerged as she lunged at him. Jun'ichi raised his sword to block her, but Gennoveffa was already raising her handgun.

A thunderous shot rang out.

The bullet sliced through the woman's skull and she dropped beside Jun'ichi, left arm outstretched and split in two where the blade had sprouted from. Her eyes were wide open, an unending stare boring into a mound of snow beside her. Her light tattoos flickered, then faded to black.

David and Maf got out of the car.

"[Fuck,]" Maf said, "[I asked you not to kill her.]"

Gennoveffa shrugged. "[She didn't leave us much choice.]"

"Even if she didn't die this way," David said, "it wasn't going to end well. She was overloading, overclocking—whatever you want to call it. She *planned* on fighting to the death. Even if she won, her body would have been devastated. There's no coming back once you decide to push your mods past their limits like that. They'll ruin you, body and mind."

David realized that Gennoveffa was holding her arm. Blood ran down her fingers and dripped off her elbow. "Oh, shit, are you hurt?" he asked.

"[Yes, but I'll be fine. One of her bullets grazed me. I got lucky.]"

Maf cocked her head. "[Either way, you'll want to get that bandaged up.]"

"[Police,]" Jun'ichi said, wiping blood off his katana with the woman's shirt.

Sure enough, the sirens were getting louder. It was only a matter of time before they zeroed in on them. People would have heard those gunshots all around town.

"Just a second," Maf said.

She kneeled beside the one-handed corpse and pulled out her hard wire. She plugged it into a port on the side of the Heredes woman's head, just above the bullet's exit wound, and began to dig through her memories, downloading files from her external memory.

The sirens began to pick up. The police were narrowing in on their position. It wouldn't be much longer. Jun'ichi put his sword away and got back into the driver's seat. Gennoveffa had pulled out a first-aid kit from the trunk and placed a bandage on her arm. It adhered to her skin instantly.

"Maf," David shouted, "it's time to go."

She ejected the hard wire. As it snapped back into her wrist, her eyes went back to normal.

"Any good reading?"

"Most of it looks corrupted, probably because of that damn shot to the head." She stood up, stumbling slightly.

"Hey." David steadied her by the arm. More quietly, he asked, "You okay?"

"I'm fine. I just... I saw her last memories. I tried to avoid them, but David, I could feel her dying." She took a deep breath. "Maybe I'll finally get that therapist. Later, though. First, I'll need some time to see if I can reconstruct anything from the Heredes' memories."

"Alright," David said, opening the door for her. Once they were both in the car, he opened his mouth to tell Jun'ichi to drive—but the Tigre was already speeding away from the scene.

Chapter 03

The Tigres dropped off David and Maf at their place, then disappeared back into the city. Maf went straight to their office, sat at her laptop, and took it offline. She jacked in with her hard wire and uploaded everything she'd found at the clinic and in the driver's external memory. It would take some time to decipher it all. She worked these problems through best on her own, so David brewed her a cup of coffee and began cleaning up the kitchen.

Most of the junk left over from the Rivoluzionari safehouse found its way into the neighborhood's recycling bin, but he set aside a small box of things that he might be able to sell. Gear that was new enough or only had minimal damage. It wouldn't fetch a high price, but at least they could make a little extra off the work.

As he cleaned up, David worried about what everything meant. Hayasaka Hachirō had likely been involved with the Rivoluzionari, he'd definitely stolen money from the Tigres, and now the Heredes seemed to be involved. Or, they would be now that Gennoveffa had killed one of them. They wouldn't just let that go. The case seemed to be getting more complicated by the second.

Once the kitchen was cleaned up, David began working on lunch. He broke an egg, crumbled crackers, diced vegetables, and added a pound of ground tuna. He mixed it together with some salt and pepper, Dijon mustard, and Kashmiri chili powder. Within the hour, he'd pan fried two tuna burgers and garnished them with sautéed greens and tomato. David preferred beef, but that was hard to come by, especially in Italy. And tuna was better than tofu.

Before he finished, David poured two glasses of water, putting a purification tablet into each. They were still dissolving when he brought the meal into the office.

"Did you make tuna?" Maf asked. Her eyes were still on the laptop, but she smelled the air like a bloodhound.

"Tuna burgers." He cleared a spot and set the platter and some extra plates on her desk.

"Oh, with [chicory?]"

"Chicory, tomato, and a little spice in the patty."

"Thank you," she said, and took a bite. Her eyes widened for a moment. "Fuck me, that's good."

"You dripped a bit on your lap."

She glanced down at where some juice from the patty had fallen onto her. "[Dammit.]"

David handed her one of the plates he'd brought.

"A bit late, don't you think?" she asked, and took another bite.

David shrugged and took his own burger, holding his plate beneath it. "Find anything yet?"

"The clinic's records look above board, more or less. I can't find any records that show they were working with Hachirō or the Rivoluzionari. Then I tried for the Heredes—nothing. I'll need more time to run a search on the names and orders that I *did* find. One of them might be tied to Hachirō somehow—a former coworker or personal connection—but so far nothing's jumping out at me.

"The driver's memories, on the other hand, are interesting. I don't think they're actually corrupted. I think that they're just hidden, like some kind of cypher or lock was added after she died. If I can find a way past that, I should get access to, well, whatever is *actually* left. The memories are still damaged from that shot, don't get me wrong, but I think there's a chance we can still learn something from them. Even if there's no info on our thief, we may learn what the Heredes are up to, which could be helpful if they show up again."

"The Rivoluzionari use cyphers to communicate. Not just their colored rags in the Real, but also in written messages. Remember the papers that I found in those tunnels where that boy from Calanchi had gone?"

"We gave all that to Quintino, though. I doubt the police will let us have another look. They've made it clear they don't like us meddling in things—and if they find out we were involved in what happened this morning—"

David tapped the edge of his optics, where the metal met his skin. "I saved photos of the letter."

"Oh. You didn't mention that."

"A lot's happened in the last few hours." David shrugged. "I was focused on getting the boy home and helping you with this case; figured the conspiracy theories could come later." He swirled his glass of water, letting the last of the purification tablet dissolve before he took a drink.

"It's a long shot, but if the Heredes are working *with* the Rivoluzionari—"

"Which might be the case, if Hachirō is involved with both."

"Right, so maybe they both use the same code."

"I don't have the cypher, but I can send you the photos. That might get you closer."

"Yeah, put the files on my laptop. Hard wire them, don't need that transfer showing up on anyone else's records. No telling what it could bring. Especially if the police are investigating that. Don't need them at our door while we're still making sense of all this."

"Of course," he said, putting his meal down and extending a wire from his wrist. It clicked into one of the laptop's ports.

Nothing that Maf tried could translate the Rivoluzionari's documents. There were more powerful decoding systems that she could try, but accessing them would require connecting back into the Net—possibly diving into it. Not only would that draw unwanted attention, but David couldn't interface with the Net anymore, and it made Maf sick to her stomach. Even if they were up to it, they lacked the equipment in their small home office.

Maf contacted the Tigres. Surely they had connections who could look into the documents for them. Or, perhaps somebody who could just break into the driver's memories. There was still no way of knowing if the Heredes and the Rivoluzionari were actually working together.

They met with Gennoveffa and Jun'ichi at an espresso bar inside the Poeta apartment building, one of many megastructures attached to the retaining walls which lined the city's interior and kept Civita di Bagnoregio from collapsing.

They got three espressos, and one caffè decaffeinato for Jun'ichi, and took a seat by the window. From there, David could look down on the city. Traffic flowed in every direction at once, save for the cars and bikes who'd been caught behind a garbage truck. David glanced up at the buildings across the street and a woman winked at him from a massive screen, drinking a bottle of premium Antarctic water—the Pepsi-Pata logo facing him. The graphic had writing on the side that read *pre-purified and refreshing!*

"I haven't been to this bar yet," David said to nobody in particular, taking a sip of his espresso. It was good. A little bitter, a little nutty.

"There's at least half a dozen in each megastructure," Maf said dismissively.

"[But this one,]" Jun'ichi said, "[it has a decent decaf.]"

David grinned. He would have guessed that the swordsman took his coffee black.

"[What have you got for us?]" Gennoveffa asked.

"[Right,]" Maf said. "[The data I pulled off of that driver doesn't seem to be as corrupted as I expected, but it's locked up where I can't access it. I did what I could, but it didn't make a dent. I've got it all packaged and ready to go for you.]" Maf tapped her external memory. "[We were hoping that you knew a lockpick.]"

Gennoveffa looked over at her partner and asked, "Giancarlos?"

"[Gian disappeared a month ago,]" Jun'ichi said.

"[What about Ten Fingers?]"

"[They're in London working some other job.]"

"[Shit, and Darren's in the hospital... What about the Spider?]"

Jun'ichi nodded.

"[They'll want something in return,]" Gennoveffa said.

Jun'ichi frowned. ["The Spider is our fastest option.]"

Gennoveffa took a drink. She seemed bothered by whoever the Spider—La Ragna—was. Still...

David said, "If they can get us access, Maf and I can figure out the rest. But it docsn't have to be done right away."

"No." Gennoveffa put a hand up. "[Mafalda has been working on this case for only a few days, but Mama Cinzia has been hunting Hachirō for nearly a month. If we wait too long, the trail may go cold. And I want more info on the Heredes. There are too many unanswered questions... I will contact the Spider. They will likely want to meet soon, if they agree at all, so be ready to move. And when we meet, let me do the talking.]" Her eyes lit up—flashes of the HUD on her lenses as she contacted La Ragna.

Chapter 04

In the city's center, locked behind massive retaining walls, stood an ancient Etruscan village: Civita di Bagnoregio. Without the walls, it would have collapsed long ago. People oriented themselves—if they chose not to use their lenses or optics' GPS—by looking at the nearest walls.

La Ragna worked out of Edificio d'Assisi, an office megastructure along the North Façade, just below Piazza del Vescovado. David could see the ancient town's rooftops poking out from behind the wall as they approached the sleek glass skyscraper whose back was fused with the wall.

The office itself was nothing special on the outside. It looked like any other wall-bound structure: a massive, brutalist building with seams every few floors where the modular pieces had been fitted together. Ads were still present around the lower levels, but they were broken up by each corp's neon-infused signage.

Most of the offices were run by a consortium of businesses. Gennoveffa mentioned that the Tigres had contacts with or owned shares of most, but she remained vague about which. Perhaps even she didn't know; the topic seemed to bore her when David brought it up. One thing was for certain—La Ragna was an independent agent. They worked with the Tigres as well as the police. A job was a job, and their ability to navigate the Net was so valuable that everyone wanted a piece of them. Perhaps that was how they *remained* independent, David mused. Most divers got snatched up by one government or another, made to run black ops missions or defend against them. People were still needed in the Real. He and Maf were proof of that, but all of the major conflicts happened in the Net. Most simply didn't notice the invisible wars around them until something failed or exploded. That had been David's experience during the second West Coast War. People seemed to ignore it until a Chinese diver shut down the Shasta and Oroville Dams. A tenth of California went dark. They cared quite a lot after that.

They entered Edificio d'Assisi and walked directly to the elevator. Gennoveffa jabbed a few keys and the car shook. A moment later, David felt it descend. He glanced at Maf, who gave him a reassuring nod.

David reached for his pistol, wary of what he would see when the doors opened.

Jun'ichi gripped David's wrist and gave him a hard look. He shook his head almost imperceptibly.

"Don't touch your weapon here," Gennoveffa explained. She said it in broken English, slowly. Then, in Italian, "[The Spider is a diver—they can exist anywhere in the Net—they can see just about anything. They see a foreigner like you grab your gun, they might feel you're a threat. The last person I know who spooked them, the Spider cooked all the mods in his brain. You look like you've got a lot in there, too. I don't care what firewalls you've installed. They could kill us all with little more than a thought.]"

David let go of his pistol, and Jun'ichi let go of him.

"Thanks for the warning," David said flatly. He tried not to show the unease tightening around his chest.

The elevator jolted to a stop. A beat passed, and the doors separated. They revealed a dimly lit storage cellar. Hallways and stairwells spun off in each direction. They were marked with digital screens that displayed letters and numbers, but none of it made the labyrinthine passages any clearer. Without warning, a klaxon blew, and heavy gears cranked within the walls as the nearest metal doors shut. A moment later, a separate door opened, its open maw revealing a twisting hallway that looked identical to the last.

"[This way,]" Gennoveffa said, and started down the newly revealed hall. "[The Spider shows us the path forward—or they are ushering us out of the building.]"

Along the way, David noticed the security cameras. They were small, easy to miss, hidden in corners and cracks in the walls. The same kind they used at military bases and interrogation rooms. He tried to avert his gaze and keep them from recording his face clearly. They were already in La Ragna's domain—they had probably already seen him—but it felt important that he try to withhold *something* from their prying eyes. Had his remote not been deactivated, he might have been able to glean some more information about this place and where all the surveillance led, what it was used for. Part of his unease was for his and Maf's own safety, the other part pure curiosity. Even the Tigres had seemed hesitant about coming to see La Ragna. Whatever La Ragna was, they were the first person that seemed to give Gennoveffa and Jun'ichi any pause.

David sent Maf a message. *[13:04] What's the plan if this goes sideways?*

[13:04] Run, probably.

David sighed.

Another klaxon rang in the distance. Its shriek reverberated against metal as gears clicked into place. Had the basement been designed to confuse people, or was this La Ragna's doing? It wasn't uncommon to have movable pathways in a warehouse, but this seemed excessive. Moreover, David couldn't tell if anyone else was here. Wouldn't there at least be a few security personnel, or some people coming to gather supplies for the offices above?

David desperately wanted a better plan than *run*, but he couldn't come up with anything either, and he feared that La Ragna would hear if he dared discuss their escape aloud. Perhaps they'd already tapped into his comms.

Gennoveffa led them through half a dozen halls. As they walked, hard wires began to collect along the floor and ceiling. They started small, but soon made it difficult to walk without stumbling on thick cables that merged into larger bundles. They all weaved over each other like an intricate web of metal and rubber. Gennoveffa followed them into a circular room. It appeared to have once been an auditorium or meeting room, now gutted to make room for a massive console installed in the center. It took up most of the room. Half of the wires coalesced into that system, where a dozen screens displayed camera feeds, charts, and articles. A diver, surely La Ragna, sat in front of it all. They flicked their fingers at the console with delicate precision, pressing holographic keys which only they could see, and seemed to manage everything all at once. Cameras panned, charts populated with numbers, and articles scrolled asynchronously. Yet La Ragna leaned back in their chair, hard wired into it through their arms, seemingly relaxed aside from their slight frown.

"[I love what you have done with the place,]" Gennoveffa said. Her words echoed around the room.

La Ragna spoke in Italian without turning to look at them. "[I'm glad you decided to visit, but before we discuss business, why have you brought the De Campo Private Investigators here?]"

"[We're working a case with them.]"

"[You think I don't know that?]"

La Ragna finally turned around to face them. Their age and gender were obscured by all the chrome they'd implanted into their body. Either La Ragna had made no attempt to retain their original form, or they'd embraced the ambiguity that came when so much of one's body was replaced. Their skin was a mix of synthetic wrapping with hard metal plates that folded over each other like large scales. Plates of shining gold ringed around their arms and cupped their chin. Where their eyes would have been, La Ragna had optics like David's, though theirs looked entirely inhuman—with multiple neon-red pupils. Their body reflected light from their many monitors. Red bounced off their shoulder, blue against their cheek, and yellow shone against their long, waxy hair.

La Ragna said, "[I'm not asking what you are doing with the De Campos, I'm asking why you brought them *here*. To this place.]"

Gennoveffa hesitated.

"We have something that we would like your help with," Maf said. "[It's on a shard in my exmem.]"

"[None of you considered that the file could be exported and given to the Tigres? Or you could have given them the shard? No?]" La Ragna huffed. They sounded more disappointed than angry—like a teacher scolding children. "[What's done is done, but none of you may speak of what we discuss here to anyone else. And if you try anything, I'll kill you like—]"

They snapped their metallic fingers, the soft clinking sound echoing in the silence.

La Ragna turned back to face the monitors. "[At least you've come at a convenient time. You have something to trade for my services. Well, the Tigres do. The rest of you, just don't get in the way.]"

A man's photo appeared on one of the screens. He was fairly average-looking, dressed in a simple brown suit. His body was only minimally modded, and he stood slightly slouched forward, but there was a certain look in his eyes that caught David off guard.

La Ragna continued, "[I was working with this man recently, a courier who was to deliver some codes to me. Things that my partners and I didn't want running through freely through the Net. It was going well, but the stupid bastard's gone rogue, and is hiding out just outside of Calanchi with a neural cloak—you're probably familiar with the tech, Mister De Campo.]"

David nodded. Neural cloaks became common among divers during his final years with the military. They could obscure a person's position within the Net. Even if you knew where the target was, any attacks through the Net would fail. They became widespread enough that classic drone and artillery warfare had begun to make a comeback in some parts of the world.

"[So,]" La Ragna finished, "[he's trying to sell some codes that he originally got for *me*. I need somebody to track him down and get them back. Once my codes are returned safely, I'll take a look at whatever file the De Campos want. That is my offer.]"

"[Sounds easy enough. Send the dossier,]" Gennoveffa said.

"[It's in the shard,]" La Ragna said, and nodded toward a console. A second later, a shard ejected from a port on the side. "[Remember, this is all off-Net.] That goes for all of you. Not a word of this outside of the Real, not to anyone else, and not after it's over. Better yet, go offline. Disconnect yourselves completely, if you can."

Gennoveffa stepped forward and took the shard. It was slim and red, largely unassuming. Gennoveffa pulled her hair aside and slotted it into a port on the side of her head, into her cochlear implant. The shard disappeared and her eyes flashed shades of yellow and red.

"[I've heard that name before,]" Gennoveffa said as she sorted through the dossier. "Nicolò Oberto…"

"[He's an aide to Senator Aiello,]" La Ragna said. "[He'll probably be guarded, but most of the senator's people will be with her. Especially after the Rivoluzionari's assassination attempt last week.]"

"The Rivos were behind that?" David asked. He'd thought that they were generally—although not officially—aligned with the political right.

La Ragna shrugged. "[The Rivoluzionari are anarchists. They make and break alliances when it is convenient for them, and the senator made a statement against them recently. It's good timing for us; this took some of her team's attention away from Oberto so that they could focus on keeping *her* safe. Any other questions you have are answered in the dossier, as well as a virus that you can use to disrupt his systems. It will paralyze a person, disable their mods, the works. Stays in effect long enough for you to pull the codes from their external memory.

"[Also, please do not kill Oberto. The codes have a chrysanthemum failsafe. If the person carrying them dies, everything is wiped clean. If Oberto dies, my codes are gone, and our deal is off. And if you die while carrying the codes on the way back, our deal is off. Understand?]" La Ragna grinned. "[Besides, it is better for business that Oberto lives to fear me. A little reputation is a good thing.]"

"[Track down Oberto, upload the virus, grab the codes. That's it?]" Gennoveffa asked.

"[Yes, and the sooner the better. Before he can sell them. I believe he has a buyer already. I can think of no other reason for Oberto to stab me in the back like this.]"

"[We'll go now, then.]"

Gennoveffa turned on her heel and walked back the way they'd come.

David took one more look around La Ragna's den. It felt strange, being roped into a plot against a senator's aide so quickly. The Tigres just accepted La Ragna's word as command. What deal did they have with Mama Cinzia? Or was this something that Gennoveffa and Jun'ichi did on the side? David would likely never know, but it was a discomforting thought.

"David," Maf hissed at him. She was already at the room's entrance.

Beside her, Gennoveffa glared at him.

David walked after them, following Gennoveffa back to the elevator.

46

Chapter 05

DAVID FELT INCREDIBLY OUT of place. The Tigres had dragged both him and Maf along, though this was undoubtedly a *Tigres* mission. David wished they could have simply stayed away. He had no love for the senator, but he also had no interest in being around when their aide was assaulted. Working with the Tigres to locate a missing person was one thing, but this... David just hoped that La Ragna was worth it, and that he and Maf wouldn't be caught on camera. He inched away from the car's window so that he might avoid any traffic cams and messaged Maf to do the same.

Jun'ichi glanced back at them through the rear-view mirror then returned his attention to the road.

La Ragna's shard contained an unlabeled ping on the map. They followed it, passing through Calanchi until they reached Villaggi Lontani, where the city's most wealthy residents hid away behind manicured treelines and iron gates. Small villas extended off the main road, long driveways leading into garages made to fit collections of cars. They were twentieth- and twenty-first century homes updated with tech from the twenty-second. They were uncanny, perfect for a horror movie set. They were sleek and polished, but still vaguely resembled castles. Their roofs were lined with solar shingles and their windows had been replaced with smart glass, but most still had gas-powered generators. The world couldn't rely on old fuels any longer, but *they* could, if they wanted to. David had heard of people back home in Upper New York hosting parties, dressing up, and fueling the house with oil from the Weddell Sea.

Nicolò Oberto was holed up in a villa on the fringes of Villaggi Lontani, atop a hill far from the city. A sparse forest encroached upon it from all sides. David almost missed the security cameras lining the walls, tucked away in dark corners. Gennoveffa said they were all connected to their own system, cut off from any outside grid. That, alongside the neural cloak, explained why La Ragna couldn't target Nicolò themself.

Jun'ichi drove past the villa's entrance. He found a spot just down the hill with a wide shoulder, and parked there. As the vehicle came to a stop, Gennoveffa's eyes were alight. She was looking at something on her lens—probably details from the dossier. If she was sharing any of it with her partner, she was doing so entirely through text.

"[One of you will come with us,]" Jun'ichi said.

David started, "I don't—"

"[One of you will come with us,]" Jun'ichi repeated. His tone didn't change or waver. "[The other will stay in the car. Eight minutes after we leave, start the engine. Be ready to drive. If we can't get out quietly, Oberto's guards will be in pursuit.]"

"[La Ragna's intel says they have drones as well,]" Gennoveffa said.

"[Drones would tear this car apart,]" Maf said.

Jun'ichi nodded, his brow creased.

"[We'll have to try to get on the road before Oberto can release them,]" Gennoveffa said. "[Or shoot the bots before they get too close. This model has a short-range EMP. One hit and our engine will go dark.]"

"[I'll stay behind,]" Maf said. "David [didn't even have a car until he left New York. I wouldn't trust him to outrun a scooter properly, let alone drones.] Sorry." She gripped his hand tightly.

[14:10] Don't worry, I can do this, her message appeared across his lens.

"[Alright,]" Gennoveffa said. "[David, you know how to use that gun, yes?]"

"I'd rather not have to."

"[I also would rather you didn't,]" Jun'ichi said. "[You are to stay out of the way, as La Ragna instructed,]"

Gennoveffa added, "[But in an emergency, it would be helpful to have somebody watching our exit. We need this to go off well to get the Spider's help—and we need their help. If things get bad, aim for the knees. Rich fucks like this have layered wraps. Golden stuff, same as Jun'ichi's got.]" She tapped a fist against her partner's chest playfully—though her expression was dead serious. "[A bullet square to the chest will knock the wind out of them, but they'll keep coming. If they're wearing kevlar, forget it. You'd just be wasting bullets. Joints are less well defended, though. Some of their mods may be exposed as well, stuff that didn't fit under the skin.]"

"[Or shoot them in the head,]" Jun'ichi said flatly.

"Got it," David said. It felt as though something were caught in his throat.

He looked at Maf and she squeezed his hand.

"I'll just aim for the head." He shrugged cynically. "How hard could that be?"

Maf kissed him, told them all good luck, and got into the driver's seat. Jun'ichi briefly showed her how to start the car, and then they set off up the hill toward the villa. The Tigres went first, and David followed about thirty paces behind. That was fine by him. If this went sideways, and it probably would, he planned to be the first out.

If it went sideways fast enough, Oberto's guard might not even notice him.

There was no path up the hill. It was a tumble of rocks and fallen branches, some rotting under the thin layers of snow and leaves that crunched underfoot. Gennoveffa led the way, and the other two followed in her footsteps. That helped reduce noise, but they weren't going to sneak into the complex unless absolutely nobody was watching that side of the place. With the reduced guard, David supposed that was possible, but a deficiency of manpower could be offset by myriad sensors and cameras. He couldn't spot any as they crested the hill and the villa came back into view, but that didn't mean they didn't exist.

The Tigres veered right, sticking to the trees as they approached one of the buildings in the back. As instructed, David stayed back. He chose to travel closer to the road, where he wasn't quite as exposed. He could only see rooftops from that angle, and a few pigeons who stood upon them.

When they reached a long wing of the main building, Gennoveffa tapped something on the side of her head, waited a moment, then approached one of the windows. Jun'ichi joined her, standing on the opposite side and drawing his knife. He pried open a port beside it and Gennoveffa extended a hard wire from her wrist and jacked in. Her eyes flickered yellow, and an audible *click* filled the quiet. She retracted the wire and let it snap back into her wrist as Jun'ichi opened the window. Once he was inside, he drew his sword and waited for Gennoveffa to join him. As she did, David received a message from her.

[14:26] Watch our exit.

David remained amongst the trees, low to the ground, and watched the window. The Tigres' figures faded into the villa's darkness. Behind him, the occasional bus or car sped past, oblivious to their raid.

Chapter 06

JUN'ICHI DREW HIS KATANA. The blade shimmered in the dim light of the storage room. It was filled with old furniture, clothes, and unlabeled boxes. There were no cameras, no alarms, and nobody else inside—though he could hear the muffled voices of at least two men talking somewhere deeper in the building.

He motioned for Gennoveffa to follow, and she slipped in through the window behind him. As she did, text appeared across his lens in Japanese.

[14:26] David is watching our exit.

Hopefully, they wouldn't need the former soldier. Jun'ichi wasn't sure that the old man had it in him to follow through on a job like this if it got messy. His discomfort in the car had been clear as a summer day.

Jun'ichi gripped his blade, anticipating what lay beyond the storage room's door. He had been wary of seeking La Ragna's help, but they would help the investigators find Hayasaka Hachirō, and that was all that mattered. Besides, stealing from a thief like Nicolò Oberto had a certain allure. Even if it was *for* another thief. It reminded him of how, in Matsumoto, Jun'ichi had taken his sensei's katana back from a craftsman who attempted to sell the blade and slip away in the night. Jun'ichi had delighted at the surprise on the liar's face when he realized he'd been found out.

It was turning out to be a good day.

Jun'ichi took his position beside the door. It was analog, with a bolt lock on the inside. They were fortunate to be on the side where they could simply slide the bolt out of place—Gennoveffa wouldn't have been able to hack into it the way she had with the smart window.

Gennoveffa counted down on her fingers: *san, ni, ichi...*

She opened the door and walked forward slowly, keeping a hand on the handle so as not to let the door slam into the wall. Jun'ichi kept his blade ready, inching through the villa, checking each room that he passed. So far, they were all clear. Gennoveffa watched his back, her pistol raised.

The villa was not as lavish as Jun'ichi had expected. The walls were painted a drab beige, and the furnishings appeared just new enough to avoid being valued as antiques. It almost looked like a regular home out of Calanchi—albeit a very large one—aside from the paintings. Dozens of them hung on the walls, seemingly made of real oil paints on canvas. Some were portraits of people; others were landscapes of the Italian coastline or the Apennine Mountains. Some had begun to crack and fade, making them look centuries old.

The hallway led to a large sitting room. A couch and several chairs, some black and some white, were positioned around a coffee table. The table supported a small stack of books, all bearing some form of water damage. A bronze skull laid upon them like a paperweight. A thin layer of dust rested atop it.

In the other room, a man spoke in Italian, catching Jun'ichi's attention. He was muttering, too quiet and distant for his lenses to translate it into Japanese.

Jun'ichi readied himself beside the entryway. A flap raised from his upper arm, a small camera attached to the end. It was an old piece of chrome, but it had gotten him out of more than one problematic situation. The camera's feed appeared in the corner of his HUD. The next room was a kitchen, lit brightly thanks to a large set of windows along one wall. Two men were arguing. No guards were in view, except for a few beyond the room's large windows, standing around the villa's driveway.

The taller man spoke a little louder. "[—it. There's still time to fix this. Just let me deliver the goods to La Ragna and we can forget all this happened. You'll go back to obscurity, and I'll—]"

"[They're already on the way,]" the shorter of the two interjected. Oberto. He was dressed in a simple brown suit, and his body sported only the most essential mods: a cochlear implant and hard wire. He leaned toward the taller man and said, "[If you can't pull yourself together... I can't have you here when they arrive.]"

Jun'ichi sent Gennoveffa a message: *[14:29] Do you want to wait to see who they're dealing with?*

[14:29] No. Spider just wants the codes back. Better to finish the job before backup arrives.

He nodded, and angled his camera to get a better look around the room. There were countertops, grocery bags, and more in the way. It was difficult to get an exact idea of the layout, but he had seen enough, and sent a photo of it to Gennoveffa. This was as good a chance as they could probably hope for.

Jun'ichi reattached the metallic wing on his arm, the camera slotting perfectly just below his shoulder. The feed on his HUD disappeared. The camera made a faint clicking sound as it snapped back into his shoulder.

Gennoveffa glared at him.

The men in the kitchen whispered in hushed tones. A moment passed, then they spoke more quickly and began to move something. The hiss of a coat rubbing against itself, the click of a data pin being slotted into a port.

Gennoveffa counted down silently and quickly. Jun'ichi watched her lips as she mouthed *tre, due—*

A piece of the wall next to Jun'ichi splintered as a gunshot echoed through the villa. One of the Italian men shouted. Gennoveffa was already advancing on them, ducking below a counter as she closed the distance. Jun'ichi followed her lead and charged from the other side of the counter. Oberto fired his pistol at them. His tall friend raised their arms to block Jun'ichi's katana and his skin shimmered in hexagonal patterns in the light—a dermal wrap. The sword glanced off his arms, sparks scattering where it made impact. Suddenly, Jun'ichi was the one on the defense, using his sword to block the tall man's fists. Hands were notoriously difficult to apply wraps to, so they were likely unarmored. Jun'ichi tried to take advantage of that, but the man was quick to block his attempts. He wasn't half bad, but his stance was poor. Unsteady.

Gennoveffa's voice rose above the fighting. "[Stop fucking around!]"

Jun'ichi kicked the man backward, pushing off him. They were tossed in opposite directions, and the tall man stumbled against the fridge. As Jun'ichi landed, he drew his pistol and fired. One bullet lodged into the man's arm, denting the wrap around it. The other drew blood, running down his shoulder.

Jun'ichi delivered another swift kick across the man's face and he went limp.

"[Security's on the way,]" Gennoveffa said.

She had tackled Oberto and hard wired herself into his temporal port. A wire connected her wrist to the side of his head. With her other arm, she kept him in a tight chokehold, even though the man looked catatonic. His eyes had rolled back into his head, and his jaw was slack as Gennoveffa dug through the data stored in his external memory. Both of their eyes flickered in unison.

Jun'ichi put himself between Gennoverffa and the main entrance. Somebody called to check in, a faint tinny sound that swelled from the tall man's ear. After a moment of silence, some of Oberto's guard began to run toward them.

"How much time do you require?" he asked in Japanese.

"[Another minute, maybe two.]"

He nodded. As one of the guards approached, Jun'ichi opened fire through the door, the rail mod on his pistol giving the bullets enough speed to break through it. After emptying half of his clip, Jun'ichi ducked behind the wall as a volley of bullets shredded the doorway. They crashed into the wall that he leaned against, wood and brick shuddering under the onslaught, but it was too thick for the guards' old-fashioned firearms to pierce. The guns were devastating to the body, but they struggled against modern armor. Even the smart glass windows held them off, though most of the panels were white with cracks that stretched across like spider webs. Jun'ichi wasn't sure how much longer they would hold.

The shooting stopped for a moment and one of the guards shouted at them in Italian. Jun'ichi didn't quite catch what they were trying to say—frankly, he didn't care all that much. They were almost finished, anyway. He reloaded, glancing over at Gennoveffa. She was still leaning over Oberto, her eyes a storm as she worked. She no longer bothered to restrain the man.

A car rumbled into the villa. Jun'ichi glimpsed it through a window, between several cracks. It was a black Lincoln, with one driver and one passenger. The passenger's arm was pressed against the window, a tattoo glowing bright blue and snaking up her arms into a crown.

"The Heredes are here."

"[Again? What the fuck are they doing here?]"

Jun'ichi shrugged.

"[Whatever, I'm almost... I'm done.]" Gennoveffa ejected her cable from Oberto's head and it snapped back into her wrist. "[Let's go.]"

Jun'ichi sheathed his katana. As Oberto's guard advanced, he and Gennoveffa were already running toward the window in the storage room.

Chapter 07

DAVID HEARD GUNSHOTS COME from inside the villa. He gripped his pistol and ducked lower to the ground, offering a prayer that he wouldn't have to shoot anyone. He'd never been too sure of religion—his family had never given it much thought in the first place—but he figured if God was listening anywhere, it was probably to the Italians. Hopefully not just the native Italians.

The firing stopped just as quickly as it started. Then, after a brief pause, there was an eruption of gunfire and splintering wood and heavy lead-core bullets ricocheting off metal and glass.

"Goddammit," David muttered, muscles aching, ready to run at a moment's notice.

[14:32] What's going on? Maf messaged him.

[14:32] I don't know.

It was agonizing to hear the war on the other side of the villa and not be able to see anything—to do anything. Not that David could or should have even tried. The less attached he and Maf were to this business, the better. He'd expected the Tigres to attract trouble, but this was already beyond anything he could have imagined. It sounded like they'd pissed off an army.

David adjusted his grip on his pistol again, conscious of the sweat accumulating on his palm. He took a deep breath, trying to calm his nerves. He'd been through worse.

The Tigres re-emerged, leaping through the window. Their shoes skid on the snow as they made for the car. David followed them. His breath streamed white into the air, dissolving. He'd only been running for a few seconds when shots fired from behind them. They were close. Something cracked. Was it a branch that somebody stepped on, or had a bullet snapped it off? More shots. David took deep breaths. He wanted to look around and get his bearings. He kept his head down, watching the uneven ground. One slip could spell his end. But should he run straight to the car? Were the villa guards moving to head them off? David tripped over a stone hidden in the snow and tumbled down the hill. He tucked himself into a ball and rolled, lifting himself up, a bit dizzy. His hand was light—he'd dropped his pistol. No time. Run.

They all arrived at the car around the same time. David leapt into the back seat with Jun'ichi, while Gennoveffa took the front passenger seat. Maf was accelerating away before their doors had all closed.

"[Turn around,]" Gennoveffa shouted.

"What?" Maf asked.

"[I want to see what the Heredes are doing here.]"

"The Heredes?" David asked.

Jun'ichi shot him a look and shrugged.

Maf rounded a wide turn. She said, "[I'm not turning around. You barely escaped.]"

"[Why were they here?]" Gennoveffa asked, her voice a low growl. "[What the hell did the Spider send us to collect?]"

"[Ask them,]" Jun'ichi said, a light in the corner of his eyes. A rod hung off his shoulder and out the window, a round bauble on the end. It snapped back into his body and the light over his eyes blinked away. "[We are being followed.]"

A humming noise, quiet at first, became louder as it approached. David twisted around to look out the rear window. A black car was following them, and from the passenger's window emerged two small drones. They looked a bit dated, modified with heavy equipment. The EMP. As the passenger reached out to loose another drone, David saw their arm, inked with a light tattoo of a crown.

"[Don't let them near the car!]" Maf shouted.

"I lost my pistol," David said.

Maf unholstered hers and threw it back at him, her eyes never leaving the road. It hit David in his shoulder.

"Thanks," he said, fumbling for it.

A moment after the Tigres took their shots, David flicked the safety off. He leaned out his window and fired on the nearest drone. Sparks erupted off it and the machine wobbled, but remained in the air.

A pistol emerged from the black car's window. David retreated back into his seat just as they returned fire. The rear window took a few hits, then shattered. Shards of glass showered the car's interior, catching in the folds of David's coat as a fierce wind rattled inside the cabin.

David took a deep breath and leaned back out, taking another couple of shots at the drone approaching his side. This time it dropped. The car following them rocked as one of its wheels went over the drone's wreckage. As it did, David saw a flash of light. The black car swerved and ran off the road into a tree. He couldn't see the wreck as Maf turned another corner, but he could hear metal and glass crumbling, even through the sound of air rushing through their open and damaged windows.

Gennoveffa said, "[Now, we turn back around. The drones are all down, their car is crashed; I want to have a word with the

Heredes.]" Then, to Jun'ichi, "[Don't dismember anyone—it only pisses them off.]"

He shrugged. "[I'll just stay in the car.]"

Maf slowed down and found a spot to turn the car around. She muttered something under her breath and made her way toward the wreck.

"I never got a chance to ask," David said as they approached the Heredes. "Did you two do what you needed to at the villa?"

"[Yes,]" Gennoveffa said, spitting the word out.

"Oh. That's good."

Chapter 08

As they approached the crashed car, the Heredes had already gotten it working again. Either its engine was strong, or the drones' EMP had been less powerful than they thought. David expected another chase, but the Heredes stood around the car watching them pull over, seemingly unconcerned.

Jun'ichi and Maf waited in the car. In a pinch, they could serve as covering fire and getaway driver respectively. Jun'ichi only had his pistol, but the way he hard wired it into his arm and handled it with such confidence made David think it might be as good as a sniper rifle in his hands.

As David and Gennoveffa got out of the car, one of the Heredes put a hand on the pistol holstered at his side. The other one, a tall woman of mixed Japanese heritage, simply watched them walk down the hill. Her gaze was ice and steel. A lioness watching her prey step into a trap. She had a slim face, dark brown hair, and a scar on her upper lip. She wore a black coat, under which David caught glimpses of her chest and arms—all decked out in chrome. It wasn't the usual type of metal and plastic wear; it was engineered to resemble her natural skin in every way save for the deep purple color—almost black. It seemed to flex under pressure, and was even textured to look as though it were porous. He thought he saw the top of a hard plate emerging from beneath her collar, too. Typically, that kind of Real armor was reserved for an army's vanguard or special forces.

David ran a scan, trying to determine what else she had installed, but most of it was blocked. Blue text appeared over his HUD that read out a few basic mods: a cochlear implant, external memory, a biomonitor... Clearly she was packing more than those, though. If nothing else, something was disrupting his optics' scans. The woman adjusted her scarf to cover more of her chest, hiding all evidence of her armor, as if she knew he'd been trying to scan her.

"[Sorry about that,]" Gennoveffa told the woman as they came near, gesturing toward the tree they'd plowed into. Considering the circumstances, the car didn't look too badly damaged.

The woman watched them closely, a grin forming on the corner of her lips. She eyed the light tattoo peeking out from Gennoveffa's coat. "[It's funny, all I wanted was to talk with you. Not quite how I expected it, but it seems everything has worked out.]"

"[If you only wanted to talk, why send drones after us?]"

"[Because you assaulted my contact. And that car of yours was spotted leaving the scene of Feliciana's murder the other day. I don't suppose you know anything about that? She was a close friend of mine.]"

"Feliciana?"

She nodded. "[That was her name. I didn't tell her family about the way you murdered her. They didn't need to know how brutal it was. But they will have gotten the body by now. They will have seen what you did to her hand.]"

Gennoveffa thought for a moment. "[If you give me her family's name, I will send my condolences and a little offering to help ease their troubles.]"

The woman laughed. "[They wouldn't accept money from you. Besides, I wouldn't fall for such a juvenile trick. Good try, though. You're welcome to dig that up on your own, but they'll be long gone by then. They've decided to skip town.]"

"[Worth a shot.]"

"[Who's your quiet friend, by the way?]"

Before David got a chance to speak, Gennoveffa said, "[None of your business. Now, tell me what's going on with the Heredes. I thought you had left Italy. Haven't seen any crowns around here for years, and now you're getting in our way. I'm beginning to take it personally.]"

"[I could say the same of the Tigres' getting in *our* way. I came to purchase some information that Nicolò had. Codes to a facility in Montefiascone. They were stolen from his memory. I don't care about him, but I still want those codes. I'll offer you the same deal: sixty-thousand euros.]"

"[Oberto sold out for just sixty?]"

"[I can do sixty-five.]"

"[Why do you need these codes so badly?]"

The woman took on a puzzled look. "[Do you not realize what they're for? I see. You're working for somebody else, aren't you? Somebody who doesn't want people paying too much attention. Have the Tigres finally thrown in their lot with the Italian government? The Rivoluzionari?]"

Gennoveffa spat. "[The idea that you think we would stoop so low is insulting. And nothing's for sale.]"

The woman cast another glance at David. "[Everybody's got a price. What about you? You aren't branded like this one is... Even the new Tigres have a tattoo to show off.]"

"[Careful,]" Gennoveffa warned her.

The woman paid her no mind. Her eyes lit up briefly, then returned to their natural state. "[You're ex-military, United States Army. I see. So much chrome in that body, so much of it out of reach. What a shame. No matter who financed or installed all of that, it is still part of your body now. It's *yours*. I have a surgeon who can fix that for you. He's brilliant, if a bit stubborn sometimes.]"

"I don't need fixing," David said, though a part of him wanted to know more. The weight of the blade in his arm—a blade which he could no longer use—became incredibly apparent.

The Heredes woman ignored him. "[It's tragic the way your country discards their soldiers. It's no trouble at all, I'll even throw in the sixty-five thousand euros, and Hayasaka can put you back—]"

"Hayasaka Hachirō?" Gennoveffa asked, a little too excited.

The woman frowned. "[Why does his name matter? The point is that he can help your American friend recover.]"

"[Where is he?]"

"[He is helping me with a project.]"

"[Where?]"

"[Listen, are you going to sell me the codes or not?]"

"[Where is he?]" Gennoveffa gripped her pistol.

The Heredes woman smiled back. "[I'll tell you if you sell me the codes.]"

Gennoveffa grit her teeth. Had anyone other than La Ragna sent them after Oberto, David believed she would have taken the deal. But whatever La Ragna was to her—or perhaps whatever threat they posed—was too great. Gennoveffa stood stiff and mute, seemingly unable to commit to anything, her knuckles white around her pistol's grip.

The woman sighed. "[Don't waste my time, cat. If you change your mind, come to Caffè Charis in Montefiascone. You don't need to ask for me—somebody will tell me you've come.]" Then, to her driver, "[Are you ready to go?]"

"[Yes,]" he said.

"[Good. Until next time,]" she said, and got back into the damaged car.

David expected the woman and her driver to try something, but they simply turned around and sped back up the hill. All that remained of their discussion lay in tire tracks and a splintered tree.

"She said that they have Hachirō," David said. "It might be a ploy. She saw how much you wanted him—maybe they're just saying they have him as a bargaining chip. But we should at least check it out."

Gennoveffa spoke through clenched teeth. "[Jun'ichi and I must return to La Ragna. Then, we're going to Montefiasco ne.]"

Chapter 09

MAF COPIED THE ENCRYPTED files she had from the Heredes woman from the prior day—Feliciana—and uploaded it to a shard for the Tigres. Once they had it, the Tigres dropped off David and Maf a few blocks from their place, then turned around to deliver the shard to La Ragna.

David and Maf were glad to take a moment for themselves. Neither of them was particularly keen on returning to that diver's basement. They were exhausted, and they both knew that the Tigres would want to move on the Heredes soon. They knew that the Heredes had Hayasaka Hachirō, but David couldn't figure out why. The evidence of the surgeon's work with that blood clinic, which they'd traced from the Rivoluzionari safehouse, all pointed toward something completely different. Had he and Maf gotten themselves mixed up in something bigger than the revolutionaries? Were the Heredes working alongside the Rivoluzionari? Or had it all just been an accident—had the wrong clues led them to the right place?

Although, did any of that matter? Once the Tigres came back, they'd either have Hachirō's location or they'd visit that café the Heredes woman mentioned. Either way, ideally, they could finish this job by nightfall. Maybe he and Maf would go on vacation for a few days, or take some boring jobs for a change. He'd love it if somebody walked through their door because a cat was missing. A fat, slow one, implanted with a tracking chip.

David's back hurt. His legs ached. His neck was sore. He sighed and wondered again if he was getting too old for this shit.

Maf stepped out of the shower, her hair jet black and slick against her skin. She wore one towel wrapped around her body and used the other to pat dry her cochlear implant. One of the lights on it pulsed yellow.

"Your turn," she said, wrapping her hair in the towel.

David considered saying something about her tone—she sounded exhausted—but decided against it. He was tired too. It wouldn't do any good to point it out.

"Try and lay down for a minute," he said instead.

"They said they would be back in an hour, maybe less."

"Better than nothing," David said, and went into the bathroom. Lavender-scented steam still hung in the air.

Chapter 10

Jun'ichi followed Gennoveffa into one of the elevators in Edificio d'Assisi, descending once more into La Ragna's lair. The De Campos had volunteered to stay behind this time. He couldn't blame them; they hadn't exactly been welcomed with open arms before. He got the sense that although they were no strangers to a scrap, the last few hours had been a lot for them. A bit of rest would do them well. Jun'ichi wished he could have done the same. It would have been nice to go home and see his cat.

"[Good job,]" La Ragna told them before either had a chance to announce that they had returned with the codes.

"[Our deal?]" Gennoveffa prompted them, ejecting two shards from ports on the side of her head. One contained La Ragna's dossier, virus, and the codes Oberto had tried to sell. The other was everything that Mafalda De Campo had downloaded off of that Heredes woman who had been lurking around the clinic in Zepponami.

La Ragna took the shards. They inserted the dossier into a port behind their ear, and slotted Mafalda's into the console in front of them. A file appeared on one of the screens as La Ragna lowered their mask, leaning back into their chair. A low hum emitted from her as their chrome kicked into action.

"[You just need these files decrypted, right?]" they asked.

"[Decrypt it, and if you see anything about Hayasaka Hachirō or Montefiascone, ping it for us.]"

A few moments passed during which La Ragna was rigid and focused. Jun'ichi caught their jaw slack just a bit, and their fingertips twitched slightly. They must have dove into the Net. He wasn't sure why they would need to do that, but perhaps it was why Mafalda couldn't break in—it was some kind of lock that could only be accessed from the other side.

La Ragna snapped back to attention, cleared their throat, and the lights on their headset dimmed. They lifted it back up, and the humming dulled. La Ragna ejected the shard and handed it back to Gennoveffa.

"[Easy as that,]" they said.

"[You found Hachirō?]"

"[Not exactly, but I unlocked everything that wasn't corrupted, and there's a few mentions of Hayasaka Hachirō in there, though not many. I don't think this person knew him well. A few other names as well. Uesugi Ayane comes up the most. That mean anything to you? Seems she's the new leader of the Heredes.]"

"[New leader?]"

La Ragna gestured toward one of the screens, and it ran a search query. A progress bar moved quickly along the bottom, below the woman's name.

"[Not sure what happened to the Heredes in the first place, but it looks like there's been a big change. I'll have to look into it more later. I'd be curious to know as well. For the time being, I ran a trace on Ayane and—look at that.]" They pointed to one of the screens on their console, where the woman's picture appeared. It was a few years old, but her slim face and dark hair looked familiar. This was the woman who'd tried to make a deal with Oberto, then pursued them down the street. "[Seems that she's in Montefiascone. Looks like the old water treatment facility in the north end. Does that help?]"

"[That's not far from the Caffè she mentioned," Gennoveffa said to Jun'ichi. Then, to La Ragna, "We ran into her at Oberto's villa. She was his new buyer.]"

"Huh." La Ragna pulled their mask back over their eyes and maneuvered controls in the air that only they could see. After a moment, they asked, "[Did you run into any other problems, Gennoveffa?]"

"[Nothing that we couldn't handle.]"

"[If there were any complications, I do want to know about it, your pride be damned.]"

"[We got what we went for, and none of Oberto's people should know who did it. This *Ayane* followed us, and we had a talk. She tried to buy your codes off us, but we refused.]" Gennoveffa crossed her arms. "[That's it,]" she said.

La Ragna didn't turn to look at them, but with their mask on, Jun'ichi felt as though their eyes were everywhere. And they watched intently.

"[Fine. Get out, then. You have what you came for. And keep an eye out for the Heredes. No telling what they're up to.]"

After they returned to the car, Gennoveffa told Jun'ichi to disconnect from the Net. He did as she asked. Gennoveffa always had a reason for these things, even if he didn't understand them at the time. His lens flashed errors at him in the corners of his vision. He blinked them away and nodded for Gennoveffa to continue.

She spoke in English, repeating the statement so that he could understand her without his lens' translator. Without a connection to the Net, he had to piece together what she said on his own based on hazy memories of his foreign language classes from school. Eventually, he got the gist of what she'd told him: Gennoveffa had made a copy of La Ragna's virus. She'd stolen from the Spider.

"Why would you do that?" he asked in Japanese.

No lights flashed across Gennoveffa's eyes. She frowned at him, then mimed plugging something back in. Jun'ichi reconnected to the Net, and a dozen lines of text informed him of different systems coming back online—the translator among them.

"Why would you do that?" he repeated. "La Ragna will be angry."

"[I know, but you saw how quickly that just... It *worked*.]"

Gennoveffa was speaking carefully. She was worried that even here, outside of the building and alone in their car, La Ragna might be listening in. It was a fair concern, given that she'd stolen from them. And based on how they last spoke, La Ragna seemed to know—or at least be suspicious. There would be consequences. Would they retaliate against him and Gennoveffa, or all of the Tigres?

She continued, "[Mama Cinzia can't spare any backup, and we're about to walk into the Heredes' turf. The De Campo's will be there, but they aren't fighters. I don't want to go in without a little something up our sleeves and *this* is more powerful than anything in our armories. The Heredes are likely all on their own system, separate from the rest of the Net. For the most part, anyway. Same as we are with the Tigres' network.

All we need to do is upload this virus into it and they'll get cut off from each other. Or maybe it'll just take them all down for us. Either way, we need something to tip the scales. We can waltz in, grab Hachirō, and be out in a few minutes. I'm not saying it'll be easy, but this is at least a better plan than whatever we'd come up with without this.]" She gestured at the hard wire embedded in her wrist.

"Fine." Jun'ichi said. He had to admit, he preferred having La Ragna's virus than not. "Give me a copy, please. As a back-up."

"[Of course,]" she grinned.

Jun'ichi offered his arm, and she plugged her hard wire into a port on the inside of his elbow. The virus uploaded, and an orange progress bar appeared across the center of his vision. As it neared completion, another warning appeared. He blinked it away.

"[The Heredes won't know what hit them,]" Gennoveffa said, baring sharpened teeth.

"First, we should make sure La Ragna doesn't hit us for stealing this."

"[Focus on Hachirō. We can deal with the Spider later, if they prove to be a problem at all. Remember, they still need somebody to handle work in the Real from time to time. Even if they suspect something's up, they won't fuck with us. Trust me.]"

Chapter 11

DAVID AND MAF MET the Tigres at an itameshi restaurant, *Dīpu Inpakuto*. The walls were adorned with illustrations of racehorses and replica racing equipment. Gennoveffa and Jun'ichi were already at the counter. Nobody else was there. David couldn't tell if the Tigres had cleared the place out, or if they'd all just showed up during a lull.

Gennoveffa suggested the ankake spaghetti as they approached. David ordered one, and Maf got two slices of pizza. It took only a few minutes for the staff to collect everything. As they did, David noticed orange light tattoos flashing from underneath their shirt sleeves: a jaw, and the tips of bullet-shaped teeth.

When David tried to pay, Gennoveffa stopped him, and tapped her finger against the restaurant's computer. "[My treat,]" she said. "[You want something to drink?]"

"Water's great, thanks," David said.

"[Four waters,]" she told the woman taking their order.

They followed the Tigres to a booth in the back with bright red cushions. As David took a seat, he was careful not to spill his meal or glass of water, which was still hissing as the purification tablet worked its magic. This one was raspberry-flavored, dyeing the water a deep pink color. His spaghetti dish sat in a thick red sauce with pepper flakes floating in it. The noodles were mixed in with onions, bell peppers, and a few shrimp, garnished with small pieces of what appeared to be sausage.

"[Susumu is an excellent cook,]" Gennoveffa said. "[I showed Jun'ichi this place after we met. We come here before every job whether it's guard duty or shaking down somebody who pissed off the boss.]"

Jun'ichi nodded as he set his sword aside and picked up a pair of chopsticks.

"How did you two meet, anyway?" David asked, filling the silence.

Gennoveffa slid the shell off one of her shrimp. For a moment, it seemed she was going to pretend she hadn't heard the question, then she pursed her lips and must have reconsidered. "[He joined the Tigres before me. We were assigned a job together, and he helped show me the ropes, watched my back. I thought he hated me at first, then I learned he just doesn't like the sound of his own voice.]"

Jun'ichi shrugged.

"[We've worked together ever since,]" she added.

David stabbed a shrimp, noodles, and vegetable onto his fork. A quick dip in the sauce, and he fit it into his mouth. It was spicy, but the spice wasn't dominating. All of the other flavors of sweet vegetables and umami shrimp were still there too, playing off of it.

"That's good," David said, a smile on his lips. He had expected a quick bite when the Tigres suggested meeting here, not to genuinely enjoy the place. He asked Maf, "How's the pizza?"

"Good," she said through a full bite.

"Is that mayonnaise?"

She looked down at her half-eaten slice. "I think so."

"[Japanese mayonnaise,]" Jun'ichi said. "[It is much richer.]"

Gennoveffa smiled. "[This place is a godsend. There have been times when my balance was dried up, I didn't have anyone to turn to, so I'd come here for a slice or bowl of something. Susumu figured out I was broke and began slipping me scraps. Then she got me an audience with Mama Cinzia. I'd probably be dead if she hadn't taken pity on me. And I can't count the number of times Jun'ichi did the same.]"

Jun'ichi nodded and muttered something that David's translator didn't pick up.

"Well, the food's excellent," David said, uncertain how to respond to Gennoveffa's life story.

Gennoveffa dabbed the corner of her mouth with a napkin. "[Enjoy it. When you're finished, we have business to discuss .]" She nodded toward a hallway behind David. The door was marked *solo dipendenti: [employees only]*.

Jun'ichi fastened his sword back to his belt, and David finished the last of his water. They brought their plates and cups to a bin in the corner so the staff could collect them more easily. Gennoveffa stopped to thank a woman in Japanese, possibly Susumu. "[I'm so glad you and your friends enjoyed it,]" the woman replied. She smiled from ear to ear.

David and Maf followed the Tigres through the employees' door. It led into a short hallway that branched off to an emergency exit, the kitchen, and another door sealed with a biometric lock. Gennoveffa jacked into the console with the hard wire in her wrist, then placed her middle and ring fingers on a scanner. The scanner blinked yellow under her fingertips, then green. The door clicked open.

David had suspected this was a Tigres-run restaurant. The light tattoos on the staff more or less confirmed that. He hadn't expected an armory hidden behind the kitchen, though. Dozens of pistols, submachine guns, rifles, and shotguns lined the walls. A pair of grenade launchers hung on hooks in the back. Ammunition was paired with each weapon, much of it ready to go in clips and magazines, more stored in large crates. On the side of the armory were a few body mods still in their packaging and a surgical chair. Its leather padding frayed at the edges, but it was otherwise clean. On a podium in the center of the room were three mounted katanas, their blades shimmering under a yellow light.

"[Looks like Diego's busy today,]" Gennoveffa said as she led the way inside. The door closed and locked behind them. "[No big deal. We don't have time to implant anything new anyway. Gotta' hit the road before the Heredes catch on to us.]"

"[I would have liked to run a hardware diagnostic at least,]" Jun'ichi said.

"[You can just update normally, you know.]"

He shrugged. "[Caio updated his gear and went blind for a week.]"

Gennoveffa seemed to realize that David and Maf were still there. She explained, "[Not all of our mods work well with the public updates. We have people who update and improve things for us, which is great until it's not. But *usually* the public updates work fine.]"

"[You want me to update now?]" Jun'ichi asked.

"[No, not now. If it goes wrong, you might not be able to help with the Heredes.]"

He raised his hands as if to say, *exactly*.

"Hold on," Maf said. Then in Italian, "[I know you said that the Heredes have Hachirō, but what exactly are we doing? Why are we here, specifically, and what's the plan?]"

Gennoveffa picked a small submachine gun off of the wall. David didn't recognize the model, but he did notice the Opere Militari Industriali logo on the side in bold, blocky letters. They were a leader in modern firearms, rivaling even the U. S.-based MiliArms and the Barett-Herstal Group.

Gennoveffa said, "[The plan is to get Hachirō, then drag him back to Mama Cinzia. Same as ever, we just know where he is now. La Ragna decrypted everything you gave them. We got Hachirō's location and a little info on the woman in charge of the Heredes, Uesugi Ayane. I also found maps of the facility the Heredes are hiding in. We'll sneak in, deactivate their systems, grab the surgeon, and walk back out.]"

"[You say that like it'll be easy,]" David said.

"[If everything goes right, it will be.]"

"[Nothing ever works out exactly to plan. Learned that a long time ago.]"

"[No shit. That's why we came here. To pick up plan B.]" Gennoveffa laughed, and slapped the side of her gun. "[I recommend you pick out something as well. You lost your pistol at the villa, and Mafalda, well, it's time to trade up.]"

"Our contract isn't to fight the Heredes," David said.

Maf nodded. "[If you have his location, our contract is good. You can take care of collecting him yourselves.]"

"[We *believe* we have found him. You'll stay with us until we see Hachirō in the Real. Because as brilliant as La Ragna is, they are only as omniscient as the Net allows them to be. The person they claimed was Hachirō could have been anyone. David said earlier that the Heredes could be lying. I don't think that's the case anymore, but they could have killed him or sent him away still. With people like them, information ages quickly.

"[You can both stay back, but you will come with us. If Hachirō is not there, we will need you to look around and see if he ever was, where he might have been or gone. And if things go badly, you'll want a way to defend yourself. So—]" Gennoveffa waved them off toward the guns.

David grimaced at Maf. Gennoveffa was right. If Hachirō wasn't there, they would lose precious time if they didn't immediately investigate the space. If the Heredes were moving him, it would happen quickly.

Maf took a deep breath. "[Okay. You're right. I'll just...]" She picked a pistol off the wall. It was smaller than hers, but David could see a module on the side that would power up each shot. It was a railtech gun, like the Tigres both had. Depending on the material, it could punch through just about any wall. Any armor. Eventually. "[I can just take this?]"

"[You'll return it after,]" Gennoveffa said, "[but yes. Take whatever you need.]"

David picked up the pistol beside Maf's. It used old-fashioned lead rounds, similar to the Beretta he lost. He liked the weight of it, the way the grip felt in his hand. It just barely fit in his holster.

"Jun'ichi," Gennoveffa said, "[do you need anything?]"

He walked over to the pistols and took a few clips, putting them into his pockets. He picked up two more and put one in David's hand, the other in Maf's.

"[Don't get caught without spare ammunition,]" he said.

They discussed the plan over the podium of katanas. Gennoveffa hard wired herself to David and then Maf, giving each of them everything that she had on Uesugi Ayane and the floor plans of the water treatment facility where the Heredes were likely keeping Hachirō. David displayed them on his HUD while they talked.

The building was an odd choice for a base of operations. It was abandoned a year ago after it began producing contaminated drinking water—worse than what had become acceptable in recent years. While it was ripe for the taking, the place didn't offer anything of particular value to the Heredes. It required certain codes to function, which were surely the ones they'd just handed off to La Ragna. Even with them, the facility would need a lot of power to start running, and there was still the issue of the contaminated water. Should they fix all of that, they still couldn't produce water at a scale large enough to compete with the other corps. It seemed like a slow plan, and didn't seem to give them any real power or wealth that gangs like the Heredes—or Tigres for that matter—usually sought out.

Assuming they didn't actually intend to get the facility running, it was still an odd choice. That location wasn't particularly important to anyone; it was actually quite far from the urban center of Montefiascone, and it didn't offer much protection from an attack.

Either way, David still didn't see how Hachirō fit into all this. Perhaps it didn't matter. Gennoveffa was right, all they needed to do was get him out of there. The Heredes weren't his problem, and the facility was past repair anyway. He just needed to focus on the job.

Gennoveffa showed them the route that she and Jun'ichi planned to use to get inside undetected: a hatch in the rear of the building that led into the basement. It looked good, but the path ran past some areas that would likely be guarded. David found a side entrance in the plans that they could use as a plan B. If that failed, Maf pointed out a window on the ground floor that might work.

Gennoveffa was agreeable to their suggestions, marking them each as alternatives, if her hatch was too well guarded or fastened with an analog lock that they couldn't break. That was always a possibility with these old buildings. Once inside, she insisted that all they needed to do was get to a console—anything that was connected to the Heredes' communications network. She didn't expand upon that when Maf asked, but she talked about it like everything hinged on uploading something to the Heredes' private network.

While the Tigres figured out how to access the network, David and Maf planned to wait in the car. They would either go inside once the Tigres were successful, or they would provide a quick getaway if things didn't work out. In the worst-case scenario, they were to flee and call the Tigres for help. Gennoveffa indicated that Mama Cinzia would not be happy about diverting more resources to this case, but that she would give them whatever they needed should Hachirō be found. Especially if Gennoveffa and Jun'ichi were both killed.

The room got quiet when the final possibility was said aloud. David wanted to object, to find a safer way to resolve this, but he couldn't come up with anything that he liked. Still, there was one option that they hadn't tried yet.

"What if we just ask for Hachirō?" David asked. "I don't know what they need him for, but this Ayane wanted those codes that Oberto had, right? She offered Hachirō in exchange for them. What if we just accept her deal?"

"[We don't have the codes anymore,]" Gennoveffa said.

"She doesn't know that. Have Jun'ichi ready to infiltrate the facility, that can be plan B. But if she agrees to a trade, we can avoid more bloodshed. Remember, if there's a fight, Hachirō is at risk in the crossfire too."

Gennoveffa looked over at Jun'ichi, who shrugged back at her.

"I could make a trojan," Mafalda said. "It won't fool them for long, but it should look real enough for us to complete the deal and do the trade. I would just need some help from you, Gennoveffa. [You saw Oberto's codes, so you can answer some questions, tell me when it looks close enough.]"

"[How long would this take?]" Gennoveffa asked.

"[Wouldn't be the first piece of old code I mimicked. I could probably have a convincing trojan ready by tomorrow aftern oon.]"

Gennoveffa paced around the room, her submachine gun resting against her shoulder and pointed at the roof. "[I don't like waiting that long.]"

"[All this will be pointless if Hachirō is shot.]"

"[Do you not have faith in me?]"

"You're already wounded," David said, gesturing at the adhesive bandage on Gennoveffa's arm.

She sneered back at him. "[I suppose having options is good. I can give you until six tomorrow morning. Then we go to Montefiascone—with or without the trojan.]"

Maf frowned. "[I could make it work. At least on the surf ace.]"

"[That's all we need. Jun'ichi and I will accompany you back to your home. I will give you whatever you need to make this, then we will go deal with Ayane. By the time she realizes what's happened, we'll be long gone.]"

"We'll have to be careful," David told Maf. "If she finds out you're behind this, it won't be hard for Ayane to track us down. We work out of a home office and there's a neon sign in the window."

Maf nodded. "We'll stay—"

Gunshots rang out down the hall.

People screamed and glass shattered.

All of it was muffled by the closed door.

David felt a shiver run down his spine.

"[What's that?]" Maf asked.

Jun'ichi was already through the door, one hand on the pommel of his blade, the other on his pistol. Gennoveffa, Maf, and David followed him out.

The scene in the restaurant was like something out of a Western. Three people sat on bikes, parked on the other side of the restaurant's windows. Their arms were outstretched, submachine guns rattling as their bullets tore through glass and wood. Glass hung like snow in the air, glittering in the afternoon light. Entire magazines emptied in a second. Blood splattered along the walls and ceiling alike, streaks of crimson where somebody had put their hand against it and slipped. The kitchen door swung as somebody fled through the back exit. Somebody else cradled a man who'd been shot, their hand pressing on the wound as blood welled between their fingers. The woman who'd taken their order held a shotgun and returned fire back at the bikers. She looked frightened, but her hands were steady as she squeezed the trigger. A biker fell on the street as a loud blast still echoed around the room. They grasped at their own throat before going still.

Jun'ichi and Gennoveffa walked through the employee's only door and fired on the remaining two. A second biker dropped their gun and leaned forward. Blood dripped down their bike as they fled. The final one followed suit, dipping into traffic.

What they left behind was a gory scene filled with shattered glass, shredded tables, and broken tiles. Blood dripped down one of the framed illustrations which hung on the wall. Somebody was crying. Somebody else began talking on a call, speaking rapidly in Italian. Sirens rang in the distance.

Gennoveffa ran onto the street and grabbed the dead biker's wrist, rolling up their bloodstained sleeve. The light tattoo had turned off, a grey imprint on their arm that formed a crown.

Jun'ichi stormed back into the weapons room, unlocking it with his own hard wire and fingerprints. Gennoveffa stomped back toward them, a wild look in her eyes. She pointed a finger at Maf and said, "[We go tonight, not tomorrow. Now get in your fucking car before I change my mind.]"

Jun'ichi re-emerged from the armory. His pistol was holstered, and he carried a pristine white and orange grenade launcher in one hand, and a string of grenades in the other. He muttered something under his breath in Japanese.

Chapter 12

Mafalda got to work as soon as they returned to the house. She sat down at her laptop, took it off the Net, and began working on the trojan code. Gennoveffa stayed close by, occasionally answering questions about the original version she'd taken from Oberto. David wished he could help them somehow, but he'd never been the type for desk work.

At least it was almost over.

David waited in the kitchen with Jun'ichi, who had taken a spot by the window, cradling his new grenade launcher. He leaned back in an old chair from the kitchen table, which he'd dragged over to a spot where he could look out over the narrow street David lived on. It wasn't far from the traffic and noise of Via Sud, but here the people walked with their kids and dogs, or played soccer in the tiny park. A few buskers set up by the shops and played their guitars or sang. There had been more just a few weeks ago, with Christmas and the new year, but a couple were still out with open bags and coffee cups, accepting donations while they played and sang, their fingers red and breath white. It was a strange little slice of peace within the ceaseless city.

The new year had only been a few days ago. Christ, it felt like it had been months since fireworks danced over the badlands.

"Can I get you anything?" David asked.

Jun'ichi didn't move.

He tried again. "I have some water, wine..."

"[I will wait for the women to finish their work in silence,]" he said, his tone terse. Then, after a moment, "[It is possible that the Heredes followed us, David, and I will not be caught off guard again. Not by them.]"

David nodded. "I'll go up on the roof and keep a look out. It's a bit easier to see some angles from there."

Jun'ichi shifted in his seat, adjusting his grip on his grenade launcher.

"You know, I don't love seeing explosives in—"

Jun'ichi cast him a menacing look.

"Just... Careful where you point that thing. I'll be upstairs."

David left his home and found the elevator. It took him up most of the way, but he had to climb the final two stories on foot. The rooftop was occupied by vents and greenhouses, the latter kept warm thanks to some help from the heat sinks at the center of each one. Even in the middle of winter, the building's residents—those who subscribed to the gardens—had fresh bell peppers, tomatoes, and several types of leafy greens.

David found a spot beside one of the greenhouses. From there, he could see parts of Via Sud and the narrow street opposite of Jun'ichi's view downstairs. With his optics, he could zoom in without much loss in visual quality, looking people in the eyes as they passed by three blocks away. Between him and Jun'ichi, they had most angles covered. David wouldn't be able to do much from this high up should anyone from the Heredes approach, even with his borrowed pistol, but he would be able to warn the others earlier than Jun'ichi from where he played watchdog in the kitchen.

David checked the time on his HUD. 16:50. The sun was already lowering in the west, casting long shadows in the hills and through the city. In the center of Muro Etrusche, above the high retaining walls, the old stonework of Civitia di Bagnoregio took on a reddish-golden hue. Tourists walked on those ancient streets, unaware of the war brewing below them in the city. Hell, most of the locals didn't realize how dangerous things were becoming.

He leaned against the ledge and settled in for the afternoon, hoping that Maf could pull her plan together in the few short hours that Gennoveffa had given her.

The evening remained mercifully dull. David thought he saw a Heredes biker appear earlier, but they stayed on Via Sud and never showed up again. Or perhaps it was a trick of the eye.

As the hours passed, David began to feel both relieved and anxious. Soon, they would make their exit and drive to Montefiascone where the Tigres' rival had set up.

From his rooftop, David could see Lago di Bolsena, its distant waters a deep black now that the sun had set. Just beside it, a hazy glow of lights emerged from Montefiascone and Zepponami. Muro Etrusche dwarfed them with its laser billboards that reached into the clouds, advertising all manner of food, clothing, and body modifications. Every three minutes—David had timed it—the lasers by the south façade reminded everyone to drink premium Antarctic water, boasting *no tablets necessary* and signed with a Pepsi-Pata logo in the lower corner. After that came the body sculpting ad, displaying attractive nearly nude models and telling people to *sculpt yourself like Donatello*—and so on. Every forty-two minutes, the cycle began anew.

A message appeared on his HUD from Maf: *[19:37] We're done.*

David took one final look around the building and then went back down to their place on the ground floor. Maf was fixing a quick sandwich. She handed half to him and took a bite of the other.

"Thanks. You finish everything that you needed to?" he asked.

"I did what I could," Maf said. She didn't sound particularly confident.

David nodded. He took a bite of the sandwich, a BLT with maple aioli. One of his favorites from the States.

"Gennoveffa was a big help, but she's also rushed the whole thing along way too fast. If this works at all, it won't hold up for long. The way the Tigres and Heredes keep pushing each other, I worry that Ayane will be giving this code a *close* look."

David reached an arm out, and Maf walked into it. He held her tight, taking a deep breath.

"Whatever happens, you and I will stay as far away as we can."

"I'm worried about what comes after," she whispered into his chest. "Mama Cinzia could blame me if this goes badly."

"She'd be a fool to do that."

Maf chuckled. "*I* won't be the one to tell her that."

"I just might. Speaking of which, where are the Tigres?"

"Jun'ichi went to get a new car. He said something about getting one that we haven't used around the Heredes. And Gennoveffa's—"

A retching sound came from down the hall. A moment later, the toilet flushed.

"Yeah," Maf finished.

David took another bite of the sandwich. "She gonna' be alright?"

Maf shrugged.

"Alright. So, we hit the road once Jun'ichi gets back?"

"That's what Gennoveffa said."

"Fantastic."

Chapter 13

Jun'ichi returned with an old blue Subaru. It didn't seem particularly fast or safe, but at least it would conceal them. David certainly would never have expected the Tigres to use a mom van. When he got inside, David spotted armored plating along the interior of each door, and he realized the windows were made of smart glass, unable to open but resistant to most bullets. It gave him a small measure of reassurance.

Jun'ichi drove, and Gennoveffa went over the plan again. The Tigres' approach had changed slightly. They would still have one person initiate the deal with Ayane, but it would be Jun'ichi. Gennoveffa would now be the one to slip through the back entrance if he failed. Meanwhile, David and Maf would stay with the van. Gennoveffa sent Maf a ping, which would reveal itself in three hours' time, that would lead them to a Tigres' safehouse. If all went well, she or Jun'ichi would deactivate the signal before Maf got a chance to use it. If not, then they would be able to get help.

The road was quiet. There were only a few other cars on it when they reached the hills and farms between the cities. Occasionally they would spot a few extra streetlights leading off toward a barn or town. The lights and skyscrapers of Montefiascone illuminated the night as they approached, but Jun'ichi got off SR71 ahead of the main exit, toward Città del Nord, the northernmost suburb of the city. Here the streets were still mostly quiet, the rest of the city looming overhead awash in lights and muffled cacophony.

After thirty minutes, Gennoveffa got out on the edge of a field, near an old diner with boarded-up windows. The water treatment facility was a silhouette in the distance. She walked into the night without a word, carrying her submachine gun close to her chest.

Jun'ichi drove a few more minutes, then parked the van on a curb two blocks away from the water treatment facility's main entrance, down a narrow alley between a recharge station and a row of cypress trees. He took a long breath, and then walked toward the water treatment facility's front entrance. He was armed to the teeth with his sword, pistol, and grenade launcher.

"They're not going to buy it," Maf said after he was gone.

David put a hand on her knee.

Chapter 14

Jun'ichi stepped onto the long driveway that led to the old water treatment facility. The night air was cold. It clung to his skin, made all the worse due to the dermal wrap on most of his body. He rubbed his hands together, then cupped them over his mouth and blew hot air into them. His breath seeped through his fingers, white like smoke. Jun'ichi moved through it, weighed down by his personal arsenal. His pistol and sword both hung from his hips, and the grenade launcher was strapped over his back. He made a poor diplomat, but at least he was prepared for when everything blew up in their faces. Jun'ichi couldn't imagine a way this night *didn't* end in bloodshed.

During the drive, Gennoveffa warned him that Mafalda De Campo hadn't been given enough time to create a convincing trojan. It would buy *her* time, though, and Ayane would be focused on him. All Jun'ichi needed to do was draw the Heredes' attention long enough so that Gennoveffa could get inside and upload La Ragna's virus. Once that was in their communications network, they could grab Hachirō.

That was the plan, at least.

Jun'ichi was just as ready to put a bullet in Uesugi Ayane as his partner was, but if they weren't going to change the plan, he wished they'd simply given Mafalda more time. He would have kept watch through the night if he had to, and then he wouldn't have had to bullshit his way through whatever was about to happen. A part of him hoped that the Heredes would just shoot him—give him a reason to use his new launcher.

Besides, there was no guarantee that the virus would work, or that it wouldn't leak out to the public network and cause more problems. The Heredes had a private Net, but it only reached so far—just as the Tigres' was limited. No matter how much one tried to get off the grid, the public network always had a foothold, and if La Ragna's virus got out there—and it was traced back to the Tigres—it didn't matter how many people were paid off. Italy would go to war against them.

In fact, he quite liked the old plan, where *both* of them snuck inside and took out whoever was unfortunate enough to get in the way. This new one only complicated things, and put each of them at greater risk. He'd suggested as much during the drive when Gennoveffa messaged him, but she shot it down.

Maybe he should have pushed back, but it was too late now. Besides, Gennoveffa's plans always worked out in the end. He expected this one to go sideways, but he also knew that they'd make it out. They always did. He just hoped they'd make it out with Hachirō in hand.

Gennoveffa messaged him: *[20:19] I'm in position.*

He replied: *[20:20] Good luck.*

Jun'ichi didn't try to hide his presence. He approached the old facility, weaving through a crowd of the Heredes' parked cars, trucks, and motorcycles. Many had armored plating. They came in all colors, but most displayed a blue crown somewhere. A decal on the side, a sticker in the window. One of the bikes had a thin trail of blood along the side.

Jun'ichi stepped into a yellow light cast by half a dozen bulbs built into the facility's entrance. He'd made it shockingly close to the main entrance before he was spotted by the two guards who stood there. Both were armed with submachine guns. Jun'ichi recognized the model as OMI-2200s, the gun's distinguishing features being its low cost and high rate of fire, though the bullets were a low-caliber. So long as none hit him in the head, he would be fine. Probably. One of the guards shouted something at him too quickly to be translated on his lens. The man tried again, and this time part of it picked up: "[—are you?]"

They sounded frightened.

Jun'ichi raised his hands. It must have looked ridiculous, to see somebody surrendering *and* armed like an action movie hero.

Jun'ichi shouted back in Japanese, "I am here to see Uesugi Ayane."

One of the guards took a step closer, raising his weapon. "[Not another step! What the fuck do you need Ayane for?]"

Jun'ichi stood still and rolled up his sleeve, revealing a bright orange tattoo: a tiger baring bullet-shaped fangs. He repeated, "I am here to see Uesugi Ayane."

"[Goddammit. Go tell Ayane she has a guest.]"

"[You sure?]" the second guard asked. "[The cat bares his fangs.]"

"[Yeah, but he's also alone. Besides, Ayane will just kill him if he tries anything, no matter what toys he's brought us.]"

The second guard went inside.

The first adjusted his grip on his weapon. "[If you want to run, cat, I won't shoot. Now's your last chance. Ayane's been in a bad mood lately, not like I have to tell you that. Were you there when she dropped off that little gift at the restaurant you bankroll?]"

Jun'ichi glared at the man, unmoving. If he wasn't trying to buy Gennoveffa time, Jun'ichi would have shot him in the throat.

After a minute, steps approached from inside, boots falling out of unison.

The guard shrugged and said, "[Don't say I didn't warn you.]"

The doors swung open, and Ayane walked through them, her scarf catching the wind. Nearly two dozen other Heredes followed her. They formed a semicircle around Jun'ichi and pointed all manner of pistols, submachine guns, and knives in his direction. So far, this was going exactly how Gennoveffa had planned.

Ayane tossed her coat aside and gripped a katana that hung at her side. Beneath the black coat, Ayane's body was a patchwork array of metal and wires. What little skin remained was scarred or healing. Jun'ichi hadn't been able to see that before when they talked with her outside of Villaggi Lontani. She was a walking tank. The kind of creature that militaries and millionaires around the world dreamed of creating.

Jun'ichi wondered if he was looking his killer in the eyes.

"[I wasn't expecting this,]" Ayane said in Italian.

Curious. Given her heritage, Jun'ichi had assumed he'd be able to have a conversation with her in Japanese. At least then he would have been able to add some nuance to the conversation. The translations lost so much. Oh well. Perhaps he could buy some time if he 'misunderstood' some of what she was saying.

She whispered something in the ear of another Heredes, who then took a few others and moved past Jun'ichi, toward the facility's gate. Probably a scout to make sure he was alone, checking the old trees that lined the yard, now overgrown after years of neglect. They wouldn't find anything. Gennoveffa was already inside, and the De Campos were several blocks away. It was unlikely that they would cst a wide enough search to find them.

"I have brought Nicolò Oberto's codes," he said, loudly enough for all of the Heredes to hear—including those she sent away.

Ayane raised her brow at him. "[You were there, when the Tigres ran me off the road, right? I think I saw you in the car when your friends came to speak with me... I thought I asked them to meet me at Caffè Charis?]" Jun'ichi did not respond, so she continued. "[Just hours ago, the Tigres told me that Oberto's codes were not for sale, and then that rude woman threatened to shoot me. And now, you've come here. I hope you haven't come with the same dull threats. Nothing you've brought will stop me.]"

She revealed the plate of armor under her coat, then let her coat fall back over it. It was enough for him to get a better look at the model. Jun'ichi considered pointing out its flaws: weakness along the seams where the plates met, more so than recent types of exoskeletons. A trade-off for thicker plates and stronger metals. Her armor was probably five or six years old—practically ancient, but still effective.

But he kept that to himself. Gennoveffa would have told him to focus on the objective.

"I would like to trade."

"[Interesting. And what for?]"

"Hayasaka Hachirō."

The Heredes glanced at one another briefly. They knew Hachirō, Jun'ichi had no doubt. La Ragna was right, he was here. With a bit of luck... Perhaps this foolish plan would actually work.

"[What do the Tigres want Hachirō for?]"

Jun'ichi did not respond. He didn't feel she needed to know about the man's debts to Mama Cinzia, and the longer he drew out this exchange, the better.

"[I'm surprised you're willing to give up Oberto's codes for him, of all people, when just hours ago they were completely off the table. The rest of the Tigres—your partners—they approve of this?]"

Jun'ichi answered her with more silence. If she assumed he was acting alone, he was less of a threat, and of course, the longer he could delay actually showing her Mafalda's trojan. Gennoveffa told him it would fail, but he wished she could have said for how long the ruse would work. Would she notice right away, or did he have a few minutes? A few hours? Should he be ready to draw his blade, or drive to the nearest safehouse? Too much was uncertain.

"[You're not making this easy,]" Ayane said, pinching the bridge of her nose. She let go of her katana. "[Look, I can't give you anything until I see that you have the real codes. Give me those, I'll have a look, and *if* it checks out, we can talk about exchanging them for him.]"

"Do you want the codes or not?"

"[You're misreading the situation, cat. You're outnumbered. And even if you've rigged the codes with a chrysanthemum, we can make sure you stay alive long enough to break the locks. My family shoots your legs to ribbons, we bring you inside and check those codes ourselves. I would rather not make a mess, so work with me, and let us inspect them now.]"

Jun'ichi was running out of ways to stall her. He pretended like he was thinking about what she said for a while, then said, "First, show me that Hachirō is well."

Ayane sucked her teeth and glanced down at the ground. "[If your codes are real, I *will* hand over Hachirō. He doesn't particularly like it here anyway. I cannot commit to anything more.]"

Something felt wrong, but Jun'ichi was out of room to maneuver. If he didn't let them look at the codes now, he feared that they would suspect him of foul play, and make him leave. Or they'd just shoot him if they couldn't risk letting him take their precious codes away. Neither was ideal. Gennoveffa needed to hurry the fuck up.

Jun'ichi pressed a switch on the side of his head, ejecting the shard containing Maf's trojan code. He held it up against a flickering light coming off a pole by the facility's entrance.

"[Go ahead,]" Ayane told a man beside her, the driver from their last meeting.

He stepped beside Jun'ichi, took the shard, and slotted it into a port on his cochlear implant. His eyes lit up like a kaleidoscope as he dug through the trojan code. Nothing about it was made to do anything. The original code was simply a series of numbers: a key. This one was no different. It was made to resemble a similar kind of key, though it would never open anything. So long as the driver didn't look too close, or if he didn't know where to look for frays in the code's construction, they were in the clear. At least, until they tried to unlock anything with it.

The seconds scraped by. The driver stared out into the night, backlit by the light from the old water treatment facility so that he looked like a ghost. Clouds seeped from between his lips as he reviewed the code, his brow creased in an unasked question. Jun'ichi did not reach for his pistol, but he was ready to the moment that he told Ayane that the code was fake.

After a minute, the lights in his eyes flickered off, and he turned back toward Ayane.

"[It might be real,]" he said.

"[What do you mean, 'might be'?]"

"[I need more time with it, but it *looks* good. It's as old as the building, though, written in a language I'm less familiar with.]"

"[Keep looking, then. Tell me if you find anything.]"

Ayane frowned at him. She clearly hadn't been expecting that. Frankly, Jun'ichi hadn't either. It seemed that Mafalda De Campo had been wasting her talents on discount investigations and freelance beat-cop work.

Jun'ichi loosened his shoulders. He asked Ayane, "Why is the surgeon here with you?"

She thought for a moment, her brow scrunched tightly. In a moment, it was gone. She took a step forward and looked Jun'ichi up and down, assessing him, a flash of blue in the corner of her eye.

"[Hayasaka Hachirō sought us out, but he has become important to my operations here,]" she said.

Her tone had changed. It was less adversarial, more... Curious? Up close, Jun'ichi got a better look at her gear. He knew she was kitted out, that much had been clear, but the seams in her arms suggested she held other secrets just underneath her military-grade skin. That sent a shiver down his spine.

Jun'ichi let Ayane continue, listening attentively.

"[Hachirō is a surgeon now, but he started as an engineer. Did you know that? The man's brilliant; in a few weeks he took this old place from a rust pile to a *somewhat functioning* rust pile. Still behind schedule, but we're making progress at least. Got the lights on, and he's been trying to kickstart the rest of the facility.]"

Curiosity got the better of him. He asked her, "What are you doing with the place?"

Ayane grinned. "[S.I.A. used to run this place. When their balance went red, the government backed them so that they could keep providing fresh water for people. But then it became more expensive than subsidizing the production of purification tablets, and some of the equipment here began to degrade. Now the suits just import all their water from the poles. You should see them lose their mind over *north* pole water. Absolute lunatics.

"[We had a lot of options after the Heredes chose me to lead them. I didn't want to deal with the old guard's territorial wars. Late in his life, my father confessed how much he regretted sparring over city blocks and neighborhoods—all that blood and sweat over nothing. But he ran out of time to change direction. So, I decided to make a difference in his stead. We're getting this old girl back up and running. It'll serve as a source of revenue for us, while also giving back to the community.

Once everything's working as intended, we'll make sure everyone in Montefiascone and Zepponami has fresh water.]"

"So you're altruists now?" he asked, eying the Heredes' guns.

"[Suits gave this place up to rot. They should be thanking us—as should you. I don't know what you call us. Something between humanitarians and rebels, I think. Like what you cats began as. Or maybe like the Rivoluzionari now, if they had a fucking leg to stand on. We're actually going to get something done, not just preach about change.]" A few more Heredes laughed. "[Anyway, I'm sorry to say that's why I can't give you Hachirō. Not until he's finished here. Even if I could.]"

Jun'ichi crossed his arms.

"[Hachirō went missing a day ago. He'd been acting rashly, so I provided him some *incentive*, but instead he broke out. He'll be back, though. I promise you that.]"

"So you have nothing to trade with," he said, and held out a hand toward the driver for the shard.

"[We're keeping the code. If it checks out, we'll get in contact and pay you fairly—and when Hachirō returns we'll tie a pretty bow on him and give you a call. You have my word.]"

"That's all?"

"[It will have to be.]"

Ayane paused, watching him expectantly.

Jun'ichi wasn't sure what to do next. What was taking Gennoveffa so long? Perhaps it was best to leave now, while they could—before she triggered the virus. There were so many of them. He began to send her a message to tell her that Hachirō was not inside, but was interrupted by the sound of gunfire.

"[What the hell is that?]" Ayane asked.

Four of the Heredes ran toward the facility. As they reached the door, a woman—Gennoveffa—was kicked through it. The man on the other side stumbling and bloody, bullet wounds blossoming red across his chest as he stumbled to the ground, eyes flashing red.

Jun'ichi swung the grenade launcher around and pulled the trigger. A shot hit Ayane directly, knocking her to the ground and illuminating the night in a white-red flash, then darkening it with a cloud of smoke. A ringing stung Jun'ichi's ears. He squeezed the trigger again. Another hit the ground near a few of the Heredes, knocking them to the side. Other Heredes fired back, muzzle flares like strobe lights. Jun'ichi felt bullets scrape against his dermal wrap, a few catching on his chest. They burned, but they hadn't gone through.

Ayane stood up, visibly shaken, a seething rage in her eyes. The blast had knocked her backward, directly into Gennoveffa's path as she struggled to make her escape. Gennoveffa raised her pistol and swore at the Heredes. Jun'ichi ran toward her to hold Ayane off, but she drew her blade and swung all in one fluid motion—faster than either he or Gennoveffa could react.

Gennoveffa's body fell limp in the snow, a long gash across her chest.

Ayane flicked her blood off the katana, sending drops of crimson across the snow, and leveled the sword at Jun'ichi as Gennoveffa collapsed behind her.

Jun'ichi launched the rest of his grenades, filling the space between them with explosions. He screamed at Ayane, but he could not hear it. He could not hear anything other than the ringing in his ears. Snow was replaced with mud and gore. It was impossible to tell if he'd hit anyone through the wall of grey smoke he'd made, but Jun'ichi could still feel bullets striking the cars around him, his body, threatening to crack his wrap. He threw the launcher on the ground and drew his pistol, then fired that until his magazine ran dry. As the smoke began to clear, he holstered the gun and ran, using the Heredes' armored cars and trucks as cover, keeping his head low, breathless as he sprinted toward the road.

Chapter 15

DAVID SAT IN THE back of the van, staring out at the dark alley. Everything was quiet and still. Not even a breeze stirred the snow-dusted trees. Enough time had passed; Jun'ichi and Gennoveffa should have reached the water treatment facility. He hoped that they could settle this all here and now, but just in case, Maf sat ahead of him in the driver's seat. She rubbed her arms as if she were cold, but she was wearing two layers of coats already. Besides, it was fairly warm, as much as an Italian winter could be.

David put a hand on her shoulder. "Hey," he said, "everything's going to be okay."

"I have no love for the Tigres. You know that. But those two aren't bad people."

"They're alright," David conceded.

He didn't particularly like either of them, but both had a rugged determination that he couldn't help but respect. He knew a lot of good people in the military who were like that. He'd worked closely with a few of them. Divers who were always pushing themselves, protecting U.S. interests and—mostly—each other through the Net. They were all a little bit insane, but he thought most divers were.

Maf whispered like she was at confession. "I'm worried that I've sent them to their deaths."

"What do you mean? They're the ones after Hachirō."

"The trojan was my idea, and it won't work."

"If it fails, it's only because Gennoveffa rushed you—that's on her. Not you. You know that."

Maf glanced out the window.

"Listen," David continued, "do you hear shooting? Yelling? I don't know what's going on, but if there was a problem, we'd know about it. I promise you that. Who knows, maybe everything will go according to plan, and we'll be able to wrap this up tonight."

Maf chuckled. "That's very optimistic of you."

He leaned forward and kissed her cheek.

Gunfire pierced the night. Maf and David turned to look at where it came from—past the trees, from the facility beyond. It came in a few small bursts, then all at once. Gunfire and explosions. Like a war had broken out next door. David could see the horror seeping into Maf. She steered the van back onto the road and raced toward the facility. There was no road access to the entrance that Gennoveffa took, but they weren't far from the main driveway that Jun'ichi had used. David wondered if it was worth the risk. They didn't have anything in their contract about protecting the Tigres, but he bit his tongue. There was no dissuading Maf now. Instead, David readied himself in the back of the van, drawing his borrowed pistol.

The driveway to the facility had been torn apart. Fire and smoke clung to the ground in front of the main entrance and on a few of the vehicles nearby, casting yellow and orange across the mud and snow. Half of the cars' shrill alarms rang out. Muzzle flares flashed through the smoke and a few stray shots crashed against the van. Cracks formed webs along the glass, but so far it was holding.

People were running toward them. David saw Jun'ichi first. He was sprinting down the driveway, his clothes shredded and his left arm covered in blood. The Heredes emerged out of the dark behind, running after him. More came from the trees, firing at him as he ran—then at the van. Shots hit the side, sending vibrations throughout it and cracking one of the windows.

Maf leaned over the console and opened the van's passenger door—no more than an inch. She shouted at Jun'ichi, "[Hurry!]"

At the same moment, three figures appeared on the opposite side of the van. David caught sight of them just as they opened Maf's door. One put their hands on her, and another raised their weapon. David took aim, but Maf was fighting them too, punching and kicking and driving her elbow into the nearest Heredes' gut. He couldn't get a clear shot.

David shifted to the opposite side of the van and swung open the door. A third Heredes was already there. The butt of his rifle punched across David's nose. His optics flashed and a taste of copper filled his mouth. He moved to stand up, but another hit on the back of his head sent him down onto the asphalt.

Time seemed to slow down. The fighting dulled and his optics were still glitching. Bars of color muddled his vision—white from the line in the middle of the road, yellow from Maf's tattoos, blue from the Heredes'. All of it blurred against the night.

David gripped his pistol tightly. A figure approached him and lifted his body into the van. He fell into the back seat and heard the door close behind him. His vision settled as Jun'ichi took the driver's seat. Neither Maf nor Gennoveffa were in the van. David leaned forward to see through the window facing the building. Maf was being dragged back toward the facility by a few Heredes. She was bleeding from the head, her heels dragging in the snow.

Any dizziness vanished then as David hurried toward the door and pressed down on its latch, but the door wouldn't budge. It was locked. Behind him, the opposite door clicked shut as well. He could see Maf being dragged off as more Heredes appeared, including Ayane herself, who sprayed the van with gunfire. The window David looked through cracked as a few rounds struck it.

"Let me out!" David growled.

Jun'ichi turned and slammed his foot on the accelerator, and the van lurched forward. Heredes rounded the corner and kept firing until Jun'ichi turned down a side street.

"They took Maf," David shouted. "We have to go back."

Jun'ichi steered away from the facility. This road would take them back to Muro Etrusche.

David leveled his pistol at the Tigre.

Jun'ichi raised a brow at him through the rear-view mirror.

"I will do it if you don't turn back."

"[What—]"

"No, fuck you, we're going back."

Jun'ichi merged onto SR71, the road they'd taken to get there. David could hear police sirens approaching from a distance. Maybe with their help, David could rescue Maf.

David flipped the pistol around, gripped the barrel, and swung. Jun'ichi raised a hand to catch it, but his attention was on the road, and he only slowed David down. He struck

Jun'ichi on the side of the head. The van swerved. One of the headlights flickered. David raised his arm and struck him again. Jun'ichi was conscious long enough to steer the van toward the side of the road, then went limp.

The police sped past, heading to the water treatment facility at top speed. To anyone else, it probably looked like their van was just allowing the officers to pass more easily. However, as traffic resumed, they stayed on the side of the road.

David pulled Jun'ichi out of the driver's seat and into the back. He took the Tigre's place and got the van running again, though the flickering headlight didn't come back on.

David turned the van around. They had to get back before they hurt Maf any more. If anything happened to her... David pressed harder on the accelerator, speeding past trees and farms and small homes that lined the street. He turned off SR71 at the next exit. The sirens were getting louder. Just another minute, and he'd be there.

He noticed the truck only after it was already crossing the intersection. David had the green light. He was certain of it, even as the blinding white headlights of another vehicle bore down on them. It rammed into the side of their van. Glass rained on David, catching in his hair and scraping against his wrap. He felt weightless for a moment and watched as the world pitched to one side. He spun the wheel, but his tires were in the air.

Then, a grinding, sparking crash. Then, everything went black.

Chapter 16

DAVID WAS SORE FROM neck to knee. He sat on a hard surface and something dug into his mechanical arm's wrist, restricting his movement. With every breath, his body ached and stung. Cuts littered his face and stung as he blinked at the room he found himself in, his optics adjusting to the dim light as they rebooted. He could hear the way his dermal wrap rubbed against itself where it had fractured on his left side. The pain reminded him of all that had happened the day before. Joining Maf's case, chasing the Heredes through Zepponami and Calanchi, working with La Ragna, the attack at *Dīpu Inpakuto*, and the raid on the water treatment facility. The *failed* raid. And Maf...

The bleariness faded as David's optics kicked on—back at full charge. Somebody had plugged him in while he was unconscious. The familiar pull of a cable hung off the side of his head, connected to a port there.

He pulled up the rest of his HUD with a blink. It was the following morning, 11:03. The forecast predicted a mix of rain and snow for the next two days. An ad blinked at him along the bottom of his vision, an alert about a sixth day of violent gang activity in Rome—though that kind of headline seemed to appear every week. When he tried to dismiss it, he was instead shown an article reporting stock price changes on a group of Antarctic extraction corps.

David dismissed all of it, then pulled up a map. It put him in Montefiascone at an unlabeled building in Le Mosse, quite a distance from where the crash had happened in Città del Nord. How had he crossed the city overnight? Or, more importantly, who brought him, and why? The lack of a label for the building he was in sent his heart beating faster. David took a deep breath and made an effort to stand, but handcuffs prevented him from raising his right hand far enough to do so.

He examined the cuffs. They were new, not a scratch on them, and used a tap lock mechanism—they were tied to a release code that needed to be administered by a person's touch, not unlike how wallets worked. That meant the code was probably stored on a shard in his captor's external memory or cochlear implant. If the military hadn't disabled the remote in his arm, he might have been able to steal it and free himself.

Perhaps he still could, if his captor got close enough for David to grab him with his free arm.

He pulled against the cuff harder, willing it to do *something*, but his efforts only scraped a bit of the dark grey paint off his mechanical arm, most of it around the seam on the underside. Obviously. That kind of shit only worked in the movies.

He took a deep breath and looked around the room. By most metrics, it looked like a fairly average-looking storage space. Boxes were piled high, obscuring his vision of most of the room. Some looked beaten up pretty badly, with tears and dents in the cardboard. A leak in the ceiling dripped on one stack, water slowly seeping into each box below it, a gentle rhythmic tapping filling the space. In the center of the room was a small high table, upon which David could see a few pistols and a sword—no, *Jun'ichi's* sword. One of the chairs was knocked over. Beside it, a boot.

"Hey!" David called out quietly.

A long silence followed.

"Jun'ichi?" David asked, his throat like sandpaper. He glanced up at the leak and his mouth felt even dryer.

David pressed them, "Listen, I can't tell if you're awake or not, so I'm just going to hope that you are. They've got me chained up. I assume you are too. They've cuffed me to this support beam over here. I don't think I can get out of it. Are you...?"

David listened for a reply that never came.

"Look, I know I'm probably not your favorite person right now, but we can deal with that after. We need to figure this out first. The Heredes took Maf. I didn't see Gennoveffa, so they probably have—"

"[Gennoveffa is dead,]" Jun'ichi replied from behind a stack of boxes. The boot disappeared from David's view. "[She is dead.]" he repeated, his voice breaking.

David leaned back against the beam. It vibrated when his head struck the pole.

"Fuck," he whispered.

It was almost noon when David heard steps approaching the door. He put some distance between himself and that old wooden thing. His left arm was still free, so he could perhaps throw a punch or grapple their captor if need be. That would only work if they got close, though. The handcuffs tugged at David's wrist, metal scraping against metal.

The door's lock clicked. David glanced across the room at Jun'ichi. He still couldn't see the Tigre, other than his boots, but it didn't seem like he had moved at all.

A man entered through the door. He was Japanese, probably in his early fifties, his thinning black hair pulled back into a tight bun. He wore a short and somewhat unruly beard. The man carried in a tray of food. David caught a glimpse of egg on the top of each bowl, piled on top of something else.

"[You,]" Jun'ichi said, his voice laced with venom.

The man stared back at him like a deer in headlights.

David's stomach growled. He forced himself to ignore it, and looked more closely. The man *did* look familiar. Like they'd passed each other on Via Sud before, or he'd seen him in pictures. Then it hit him: they'd been kidnapped by Hayasaka Hachirō.

David wasn't sure whether to be furious or relieved.

"[I heard the Tigres were looking for me,]" Hachirō said in Japanese, almost apologetically. Then, to David in English, "I will explain everything. But first, you must eat. Both of you. This is dry curry, the best I could find on short notice."

Hachirō placed one of the bowls in front of him. David eyed the rice, ground pork, diced vegetables, and egg. Steam rose from it lazily, and the room filled with the smell of curry powder.

Hachirō placed the other bowl in front of Jun'ichi. David caught a flash of movement and watched him kick the curry aside, spilling the bowl's contents across the floor. Grains of rice and cubes of carrot rolled across the cement.

"[I wish you hadn't done that,]" Hachirō said, staring at the spill.

"[I'm going to return you to] Mama Cinzia," Jun'ichi said.

"[We can discuss that later. For now, I need to clean up the kitchen.]" Hachirō sighed heavily. To David he said, "Please try not to spill yours."

David had been wary of the food at first, but it didn't take long for his hunger to win out. He hadn't eaten since the day before, when Maf had shared her sandwich with him. He needed to get back to her. The Heredes had already killed Gennoveffa. David didn't know what Hachirō was plotting, but he knew that he couldn't help Maf on an empty stomach.

No part of the curry tasted like poison, not that he knew what poison tasted like, but the food was just fine. He ate half of the bowl, enough to sate his hunger, and put it down on the floor. He gently pushed the rest towards Jun'ichi with his foot, careful not to knock it over.

"You need to eat," David said quietly.

Jun'ichi was within reach of it, if he only tried. He didn't move.

"It tastes fine," David said. "You want to capture this guy, right? Bring him back to the Tigres? You can't do that hungry."

Jun'ichi's mirthless chuckle echoed off the walls. "[You think so little of me, David. I have been through far worse than Hayasaka Hachirō.]"

The half-eaten bowl of curry remained between them. Slowly, less steam rose from it, until David couldn't see any at all.

Chapter 17

HACHIRŌ RETURNED, CARRYING A folding chair. Jun'ichi rattled against his chains at the sight of him. He watched the Tigre carefully, then approached David. He set up the chair, whose joints creaked at the movement. When he sat in it, Hachirō kept clear of both David's and Jun'ichi's reach.

David eyed Hachirō's left hand. His pointer finger was tipped with a familiar-looking metal implant—his wallet. His ring finger had a similar implant coated in black with a notch that matched the tap lock on the cuffs. Then he noticed the man's expression. He looked frightened. Worry lines etched into his brow and his eyes had dark shadows beneath them. The outline of a still-healing bruise poked out from underneath his shirt sleeve.

Hachirō glanced at the half-eaten bowl of curry on the floor, untouched since David had offered it to Jun'ichi. A fly walked around the rim, pausing every few seconds to engorge itself.

"David," Hachirō said, offering a slight smile. "I need to talk to both of you, but I'm not sure I'll get too far with your companion, so I'll just speak loud enough for him to hear."

David had a thousand questions: how did the surgeon know his name? Had he known that he and Maf were looking for him? He supposed that a name wasn't particularly difficult to find these days, but when had Hachirō known to look for it? The words caught in David's throat. He simply nodded, and let Hachirō continue. Whatever he wanted to talk about now, that was what mattered most to the surgeon—and David was curious what that could be.

"I'm truly sorry for all of this," Hachirō continued, gesturing to the room. "I hadn't intended to hurt anyone, but I was running out of time. In the moment... Never mind. You want to know why you're here, not to hear me ramble."

David shrugged. "No, it's no trouble. I've got time," he said, rattling his handcuff. At the same time, he blinked, and his optics began recording Hachirō. A red light pulsed in the corner of his vision. He wished he'd turned it on before the surgeon's monologue began. "Go on," David prompted him.

Hachirō nodded. "Right. Look, I'm not trying to be difficult. I will answer your questions, and the restraints are just for *my* safety. I will release you once I am confident you won't try to harm me or immediately turn me in to the Tigres."

Jun'ichi's chains rattled.

"I will go with you. But first I need your help." He took a deep breath. "I stole from the Tigres for the Rivoluzionari. I believed in their vision of a more equal Italy, but they took the money and washed their hands of me. They are no friends of the Tigres, you know, but they also were not ready to openly fight against them. Though I'll note for you, Tigre, they were happy to *spend* the money." Hachirō paused to let that sink in. "Overnight, I went from a valued member of the resistance to, well, nobody. I sought protection for myself and my son, but everyone rejected us either for fear of the Rivos or Tigres. Nobody would even take Ichiro in. And I didn't dare bring him to my sister out of fear that somebody would try to use him—or her—against me.

"That's when I ran into the Heredes. I did not tell them about the exact trouble I'd found myself in, and they did not care to ask. They offered to give us shelter in exchange for my work on this facility that they were trying to get running again. I agreed, because what else could I do?

"It was fine at first. I liked what the Heredes were doing. Ayane has a bit of a silver tongue, I think is the expression? She makes you want to be a part of her work. But the Heredes are not. The longer things took, the more irritated they became.

Ayane was always a challenge, but her lieutenants were worse. She held them back for some time, always with a lingering threat—if she was what stood between them and my family, what would happen when she was out on business? You'd better hurry up, or something bad might happen. She never said those words aloud, but the threats became less subtle over time.

"Eventually, her Lieutenants convinced her that I was lying about the challenges of getting the facility running again. They made her think that I was using them to stay hidden. She turned against me. Against me *and* Ichiro.

"Ayane moved us from our room into the basement, convinced that we would work faster if it meant we would be awarded better accommodations. Then, she threatened to kick us both out and sought alternate means of restarting the facility. Suddenly, I wasn't just trying to resurrect the facility, I was also racing against Ayane."

"That's where Oberto came in," David said. He knew the answer to his question, but he wanted Hachirō to confirm it on the recording. "Ayane went to his villa looking for codes—something that would have gotten the place running faster?"

"I believe so. She did not consult with me, I only found out about Oberto after I overheard some of the others talking about it. Those codes would have saved me a great deal of headache in restarting things. The Heredes were furious about having them stolen out from underneath them."

Hachirō looked like he had more to say about that, but he hesitated.

"I escaped that evening, just a few hours before you arrived," Hachirō said. "Things were beginning to feel not just tense, but dangerous. Their aggression was no longer just directed at me, but also at Ichiro. I could have borne the Heredes' disdain and abuse, but I could not bear seeing them use Ichiro as... As motivation. I had planned to leave with him, but we got separated and he was captured. I almost went back for him, but I am no fighter. I need to get back in there and free him. And I saw the wreckage of that place as I drove past it the other night. Not sure what exactly happened, but something tells me you two could use a chance at revenge."

David shut off his recording. "They killed his partner," he said, nodding his head toward Jun'ichi, "and they kidnapped my wife."

Hachirō nodded. "At least the Tigres are upfront with people. You always know where you stand with them. The Heredes put on a kind front, but then they use the people closest to us as leverage to get whatever they want."

"We already tried to get in. Clearly, it didn't work."

"I can help you with that," Hachirō grinned. "You have some old military-grade tech in that body of yours, yes?"

"It's not *that* old."

Hachirō waved his comment away. "I can turn it back on for you. All those old tricks you used to use, you'll have them back. And let me tell you, I've seen what the Heredes are packing. It will be tough, Ayane in particular, but with all of your mods reactivated you'll catch them off guard. Their gear is high quality for the street, but much of it doesn't compare to real military-grade mods."

David glanced down at his arms. To have all of his mods back was hard to imagine. He'd been deactivated for years now. He was a civilian. It was illegal to reactivate any of the gear that the army had put in him.

But Maf was in danger. He knew that before Hachirō described the way they used people. What would happen if he returned with Quintino and the police, or if he and Jun'ichi called for support from the Tigres? A large-scale assault on the water treatment facility might make them panic. Panicking Heredes might be even worse. But with his gear back...

"Let Jun'ichi and I *both* go, and I will help you."

"[What?]" Jun'ichi shouted.

"I need to make sure you won't pull anything during the surgery. Jun'ichi will watch over me while you rewire me."

"[I will cuff him and bring him back to Mama Cinzia,]" Jun'ichi said.

Hachirō sighed. "You see what I mean? [You always know where you stand with the Tigres.]"

"[I will cut out your tongue, Hachirō,]" Jun'ichi said, his chains straining against metal.

"I can do the surgery while you're awake," Hachirō told David. "You won't have to go under. It's actually as simple as you said, just rewiring a few things, and you're all set. If you want me to stop, if you feel uncomfortable in any way—"

"[He is a liar and a thief, David!]" Jun'ichi growled.

"—I will stop," Hachirō continued. "I can't do this alone. I can't go to the police. They will just arrest me for theft. So many are on the Tigres' payroll, and they will jump at the chance to collect a bounty. Or just Mama Cinzia's favor. I'd like to trust Jun'ichi, but even he cannot do this alone. I need you, David. I need you to help get inside, to keep me hidden from the Tigres for the time being—"

"Liar," Jun'ichi said in English, spitting the word across the floor.

His foot swung and toppled the boxes that lay between them. One opened on the way down and old magazines fell out from it, hundreds of issues of *Mensile Dipiù*, back from when they printed more than just a few collector copies. From behind where that edifice of cardboard once stood, Jun'ichi sat on the floor cuffed to a pipe that ran down from the ceiling. He pulled against his cuffs, his wrist bleeding, his dermal wrap littered with fractures and dents. A few bullets were still embedded in his chest. It was a miracle he was alive at all.

"Christ," David whispered.

"[Do not listen,]" he demanded. Then, more softly, almost pleading, "[Do not listen.]"

"They have Maf," he told Jun'ichi. "I can't let them hurt her."

"[The Tigres will help you,]" Jun'ichi said.

"How long will that take? If Gennoveffa—"

"[Do not say her name,]" he growled.

David recoiled slightly. "If they still had *her*," David ventured, "would you not do everything in your power to free her? As quickly as possible?"

Jun'ichi averted his eyes.

"I will help you, Hachirō." David kept his eyes on Jun'ichi, who slumped back against the pipe he was chained to. "But if you try anything—"

Hachirō interrupted him, his lips nearly curved into a smile. "I will stop the instant you request it. This, I promise. Your Maf, my son, even Jun'ichi's bloody revenge... As unlucky as our alliance may be, I believe it may have been fate."

Jun'ichi glared at him. Had he not been restrained, David believed he would have tackled Hachirō and dashed the surgeon's head against the concrete.

"I've never liked fate," David said, holding up his wrist with the cuff on it. "Let's get this over with."

Hachirō placed his ring finger on the cuff, and the lock clicked open. The cuff sagged around his arm and fell to the floor. A ring of silver scratches and scuffs had worn a mark into his artificial arm. When they made for the door, Jun'ichi cursed and shouted at them both, straining against his cuffs like a rabid animal.

Chapter 18

HACHIRŌ LED DAVID THROUGH an old brick hallway. The few windows had been shuttered, leaving the building dark—save for slivers of sunlight that slipped through their imperfect and weathered seams. They stepped into an open room lined with dark wooden shelves that protruded toward David like a ribcage of some dead beast. They were mostly barren. A were rotten and had collapsed onto the floor. It was a dead library, nearly hollowed out, aside from the few books forgotten by whoever cleaned out the place. No wonder the location had come up nameless on David's HUD. Hachirō had taken them to a place that—despite its physical size—no longer existed on the map.

"This is [the Le Mosse library,]" Hachirō explained. He picked up an electric lantern and twisted a knob on it, illuminating the space with a steady white light. The room arched overhead, and their footsteps echoed off the walls. Even with the lantern, shadows clung to distant halls and stairways. "An old neighbor of mine used to work here. She told me all about it. The [library] was originally a shelter, then it was converted to store books that were previously kept in flood zones. It was shuttered in 2155, right before poor Ludovica was set to retire."

"You've been hiding in plain sight all this time?"

"Only since I escaped the Heredes, just about twenty-four hours ago. I would have preferred going back to my apartment, but that's the first place they would look for me, don't you agree?"

David nodded. "That was the first place Maf looked for you."

"Maf is your partner?"

"My business partner and my wife. She worked your case solo for a few days while I was busy... It's gone to hell since then."

Hachirō took a step forward. "I am sorry that the Heredes took her, but it is good not to be alone in this. The Heredes do not have a proper place to keep prisoners. Perhaps my Ichiro and your Maf are together, keeping each other company. Keeping each other's spirits up."

He picked up a book from one of the shelves. Its cover was plain and the pages wrinkled from a long-passed flood. The title read *Ikigai*.

Hachirō continued, thumbing the worn yellow pages with a delicate touch. They crinkled and snapped under his touch. "'Ikigai' is the name of a world-famous Japanese concept, written about in a book by the same name. It means—roughly—'to live with purpose.'" He grinned at the book. "This is not *that* Ikigai. It is a fictitious tale of revenge, twisting purpose into vengeance and life into death.

"My son told me once that this version of Ikigai was just as important as the classic. It wasn't real, and it twisted the but it meant something real to him, as the original book did to me. It twisted the original meaning, but Ichiro said it did so to teach other lessons about control.

"Funnily enough, like this fiction is a mirage, so too was my book. The *Ikigai* I read when I was young was written by two Spaniards who happened to spend a few years in Japan." He chuckled. "It is so hard to tell what is truly part of my people's heritage anymore. So much of what I grew up with was created by foreigners who idolized Japan, or by the Japanese who sought to reimagine foreign works. In the wake of our diaspora, people are returning home, blending their experiences abroad with Japanese ones."

"What does—"

Hachirō put the book back on the shelf. "Truth is subjective, David. It must be made and shared, and only then can it be real. You and I have work to do. So, let us begin, and make our own truth. We shall make real our families' freedom."

"Right," David said.

"My tools are just over here."

Hachirō indicated a long wooden table where he'd left a few bags. He opened one, revealing a few surgical tools.

"I'll need to make an incision to access your mods. Likely just one, but depending on their exact make, I may need to do one for each. I'll need your help to locate them so that I don't cut more than is necessary. I only have so much medi-gel. Before we get started, I'll jack in to your cochlear and—assuming you have one installed—adjust your [nociception editing machine.]" He said the final words in Japanese. "Sorry, I try to speak English with you, but a few words have always escaped me."

"It translated fine," David reassured the surgeon, though even in English, he didn't know what it meant.

"[Good.] Excellent. With a slight adjustment, you won't feel any pain while I work on you." He pulled a hard wire from his wrist and gestured toward the side of David's head. "May I begin?"

"If we get a chance," David said, sitting on the hard table, "I want you to disable all of this stuff after we're done. The police already don't love having me around, even when they contract Maf and I to help them with a case. I don't need to give them reason to arrest me."

"If all goes as planned, you can have any favor you want of me, David."

Hachirō plugged the cord into one of David's ports, and the lenses over his eyes lit up. David wasn't sure what to expect, but he didn't feel any different after Hachirō unplugged. He made a fist, and noticed that his fingertips felt a bit numb, but that was it.

"Now let's see what we're working with," Hachirō continued, gazing off into the distance. Then, he smiled. "A double-action US-202C dagger in the right arm, [quick breach remote] in the other, and I see some network receivers and transmitters as well. Those will be the most trouble, but I think I can get them working again. Am I missing anything?"

"That's it."

"Excellent. The Heredes won't know what hit them."

Although the surgeon had explained the operation's simplicity, David was still surprised by how quickly Hachirō worked. He cut through part of David's dermal wrap and peeled a section of it away. For the first time in years, David felt a breeze on his arm. In that window of skin, Hachirō made a small incision, using what looked like a toothed pair of pliers to hold the skin back. It bled far less than David expected, and whatever he'd done when he jacked into David's cochlear implant completely removed any pain. David could feel Hachirō prodding and pushing his arm, but that was it. Still, David tried not to look too much. Watching the surgeon operate on his arm—seeing the metal and muscle and blood turned his stomach. At the same time, it was hard to look away.

Hachirō found a switch hidden below the skin, part of the remote that the U.S. military buried there back in '36. He'd only just turned nineteen when they installed it. He hadn't been awake for the procedure that time—though David guessed that implanting a mod was quite a bit different than kickstarting one already in place.

Hachirō revealed a metal lid on the remote, which he raised. A thin metal rod fell out from underneath it, and the surgeon placed it so that it held up the lid. Beneath it were myriad wires and gears, all of which appeared like they should have been moving, but were still.

The surgeon hummed as he cleaned the mod. David tried not to think about it too much, though he felt like Hachirō was testing him every time he wiped a bit of blood or gunk onto a rag he'd found. The blood made sense—Hachirō was playing auto-body shop with his arm—but some of it had substance.

"Just be honest with me," David asked after a few minutes, "is there anything in there I need to be worried about? I've heard of people whose bodies reject their mods, or become infected by them."

Hachirō smiled at him. "That would have happened years ago, if your body ever was going to reject these. Nothing to worry about. I'll be done soon."

A few minutes later, Hachirō jacked into the mod in David's arm, toggled a switch, and David's HUD flared to life. Every electrical device within his immediate area became something within his control—even the mods in Hachirō's body. The sensation—the sheer amount of information flooding his senses—was overwhelming. The lights flickered around them as he accidentally sent signals to them with his remote. Hachirō whispered for him to stop. David's HUD alerted him to devices outside of his vision: traffic cameras, computers, cars, the mods in people's bodies. All of it was in his reach, a string of points on a thread that ascended into the sky and dispersed around the world. Like beads on a necklace, intricately linked and glittering in the midday sun.

Hachirō disconnected his wire, and a few of the notifications that bombarded his HUD disappeared. What seemed like hundreds remained. David closed his eyes and took a deep breath. His HUD kept giving him alerts about other devices that entered his range, but he was able to filter out the ones that he didn't need access to. Another deep breath. He wanted to see if he could remember how the quick breach remote worked.

David's eyes remained closed, but his optics fed him a camera feed, like a vintage movie. He could see several homes, a large church, and directly below passed a long road that cut into the earth, flat stones lining parts of it. Behind the rows of old homes and shops, the city had expanded and built on top of them. None of the buildings were as impressive as anything in Muro Etrusche, but there was a clear difference between old construction and the newer, more blocky, almost American-style buildings.

He spotted another traffic camera on a streetlight, and a thin blue targeting reticle appeared over it. His view flickered, and then was replaced by something new: asphalt, cars skating across it, and patches of snow between them. He'd shifted his view onto the streetlight camera.

His HUD flared up again, a barrage of information about his new perspective. Drivers and their cars appeared and disappeared as they passed below, and the names of nearby businesses scrolled past, a few highlighted in red sponsorship banners. Boxes flickered in the distance, dozens of them.

David blinked between the city's cameras. Visions of the city, its parks, and the farms to the north appeared and disappeared. He was in between worlds: his vision flooded with that of the cameras now miles from his body, his other senses still back in the old library. The connections were built upon the Net, but he hadn't fully immersed himself in it. He could still smell the old books and hear Hachirō pleading for him to be careful just as he came within view of Rocca dei Papi. The ancient fortress became his guiding star, as most buildings near to it were constructed within sight of its stone watchtower. Weaving through the space above the city, traveling higher as he found more cameras to jump to, he felt a bit like Spider-man—although rather than swinging, he was being teleported between points. It was almost dizzying to snap through the city like that.

As he jumped further north, David became aware of a pressure in the back of his head. In the Real, he felt the hairs on his neck stand on end. Something was following him. He didn't know where from, or how he even knew, or even if it was human—but it was something he'd felt during the war. He'd probably set off some kind of alarm as he became reacquainted with the not-quite-Net. He just needed to go a bit further. He'd already crossed most of the city; a few more jumps was all he needed.

The Rocca dei Papi became obscured by rows of newer and taller buildings, so he found other means to navigate. David followed the SS2, circled the old high school, then the university. The presence trailing him neared. He could feel that pressure closing in more quickly. David jumped to a few random cameras quickly, hoping to lose it. The pressure faded briefly, but it was still close.

He wound up in an alley—the same one where Jun'ichi had left the armored van the night before. He hadn't intended to look at that spot again.

He jumped once more. This camera was angled in a way that made viewing the water treatment facility difficult, but he could still see it. There was motion outside—guards at the entrance. Four of them, and more along the side. Their bodies lit up like a Christmas tree. Points of possible connection for his remote, but the lights were all red—either out of range or too well protected to connect with. He was able to I.D. a few of the guards. The names didn't mean anything to David, but a few were listed as members of the local police. They spoke for a moment, then the officers got back in their car and left. They didn't seem to take anyone with them.

David felt a blackness erupt across his vision. The camera hadn't simply turned off; something tore him away from it.

David opened his eyes and clutched at his heart. At some point, he'd stopped breathing, and now gasped for air. The library's walls echoed the wheezing sound back at him. Hachirō put a hand up for him to be quiet, fear plastered across his pallid face.

"How long was I gone?" David breathed.

"[A few minutes,]" Hachirō said. "[I tried to wake you.]"

"I saw the facility. The Heredes were talking with the police, but it seems there were no arrests," David said, adjusting his arm. Hachirō hadn't closed it up yet. "Then something came after me. Pushed me out before I got a chance to really look around."

"The police here aren't under the Tigres' thumb the same way they are in Muro Etrusche. But that doesn't mean *nobody* has people on the inside. Or perhaps they've been convinced that the Tigres are the aggressors here.

"As for what kicked you out, [it could be anything.] The local network has automated systems designed to keep intruders out. The police have people monitoring the Net at all times. The Tigres or Heredes could have found you, too. It could have been the Spider, but they usually keep to themself, as I understand it. Unless you piss them off."

"I never went into the Net. Not fully. I could still hear this place, you."

"Good. Then whoever it was probably didn't get a clear read on you. They certainly could have found your location if you stayed much longer, but I don't think we're at any risk... Still, we should probably close your arm up and decide what to do next."

"Right."

Hachirō ran another diagnostics test to make sure all of David's mods were working properly, and that nothing had followed him back from his race across the city. He seemed satisfied at the result and shut the remote in David's arm, then began to stitch close the incisions he'd made. He applied a thick coat of medi-gel and wrapped his arm in gauze. The gel made his skin itch, but in a few days it would heal, and the gauze would keep it clean in the meantime. If he was a little lucky, none of Hachirō's work would even leave a scar.

As the surgeon cleaned his equipment, David tied his dermal wrap back together with a strip of fabric he tore off his own shirt. He tightened it around his arm as much as he could manage. It wasn't ideal, but it would hold well enough until somebody could repair it properly.

When it was finished, David sat up, still wrestling with all of the information on his HUD. He hadn't dealt with anything like it in years. David raised his mechanical arm and tried to focus on it. A moment later, his wrist opened and his hand split in two, revealing a long blade. He turned it over in a sliver of sunlight, marveling at how natural it felt even after all this time.

He had never wanted his military hardware back. It would have made some days easier, sure, but it would also put a target on his back. Strength attracted opposition, and he could think of more than a few people who wouldn't take kindly to the idea that a fully powered U.S. soldier was running around Italy. But that was a problem for later. All he needed then was to get Maf back. If he could save Hachirō's son in the process, even better.

"You look [deep in thought,]" Hachirō said.

David retracted the blade and his mechanical arm reformed. "Just trying to figure out if this is a stroke of luck, or the beginning of a disaster."

Hachirō smiled. A sadness lingered in his eyes. "I believe that I am lucky to have met you."

"But am I lucky to have met you?"

Hachirō frowned. "I cannot say."

Chapter 19

AFTER HACHIRŌ CLEANED UP his makeshift surgical table, David followed him into a small kitchenette in the basement. He tried flicking on a light, but it didn't work. Hachirō made no effort to illuminate the dark room, so David switched on his optics' night-vision mode. In the meantime, the surgeon retrieved three boxes of pre-made curry from the fridge—momentarily blinding David with its light—and put them in an old electric oven.

"I thought you made that," David said, readjusting to the dark.

"The corner store has good enough food, and it's not too expensive either. Right now, I can't afford to spend much time outside going shopping. Not with the Heredes out looking for me. This is faster." Hachirō leaned back against the oven and grinned. "Even if I could spend time out, I wouldn't torture either of you with my cooking."

"It can't be that bad."

Hachirō shook his head. "Careful, David. Optimism kills."

They ate in the dimly lit library. David mulled over how long it would be before the Heredes found them. If not them, the Tigres would eventually come looking for Gennoveffa and Jun'ichi. And then there was that *thing* following David around in the city's security network. It was probably an auto-tracer from the police. Each city had at least a few bots monitoring their systems, kicking out intruders and monitoring the people. But David didn't know if that was what pursued him. Not for sure.

When he finished eating, David picked up the third bowl of food and carried it out of the room. It was still warm to the touch, still steaming a bit.

Jun'ichi was where they'd left him, though he'd dented the pipe he was chained to, and a ring of blood lined his wrist. Shreds of his dermal wrap lay around him, peeled away from the cuffed hand.

"Jesus," David said.

Jun'ichi spat on the ground, glaring up at him.

"Look, I get that you're pissed at me, but we've got limited options right now. You know it just as well as I do. So you're going to eat this, because I need your help, and I can't have you clutching your stomach while we go back in to rescue Maf and Ichiro."

Jun'ichi sneered at him. "[Our business is finished.]"

"No it's not." David set the food down next to Jun'ichi. He ignored it. "I'm going back in. I'll try to stay unseen, but I think the Heredes have heightened their security. I need you at my back in case things go sideways."

"[There aren't many of them, and a few were injured when... How do you know they've increased security?]"

David flashed his HUD—a static of bright blue which he knew Jun'ichi could see glint across his optics—and revealed the blade in his arm. For just a moment, Jun'ichi's brow raised.

"Hachirō kept his word," David said.

"[How very kind of him.]"

"We've both got somebody in there we love."

Jun'ichi looked away.

"Look, I don't take you for the vengeful type," David continued, retracting the blade and taking a seat. The same one Hachirō had taken when he came in to negotiate with David. "In the short time I've known you, you've been nothing but professional. Like Jack Danger."

"Jack Danger?" he asked.

"From the action movies. They're big over in the U.S. It was a James Bond reboot that developed into a thing of his own—the contract killer with a heart of gold."

"[You think I have a golden heart?]"

"God, no. But I think you truly cared for Genno—"

Jun'ichi strained against his cuffs.

"Right, sorry. But I think you truly cared for *her*, not just because she was a Tigre but because of who she was. The woman with a fondness for itameshi food. I won't presume to understand anything beyond that, but it was clear you two were close. And I suspect you'd like a chance to see her plan through."

He scowled. "[The Tigres will not want to escalate this feud further. Not without more information.]"

"You're not hearing me. I'm going in to get Maf out. If I can help get Hachirō's son out too, great. I would like your help, but I don't need it."

David stared the Tigre down. Jun'ichi stared back, unflinching. The last part was a lie, but David didn't have time for games. He needed to know where Jun'ichi stood. Soon he and Hachirō would have to make a move, with or without his help.

David pressed him, "Which is it, Jun'ichi? You can either help me, or I can make sure you stay locked up until we're done."

Jun'ichi's gaze shifted toward the ground. There was a long pause before he spoke. David could hear the wind outside rattling the shutters, and honking as somebody made their way through traffic.

"[Have Hachirō release me.]"

"Does that mean you'll help?"

His eyes met David's again. A fire raged beneath them. "[If I am to help with your suicide mission, I need to know that you can watch my back as well. You may have your old toys back, but can you use them? It's been a while since you served in the military. You panicked at Oberto's villa. You have done nothing to help find Hachirō except let us get captured by him. I don't believe you can do what you are saying, David De Campo. But... If you can best me in single combat, I will consider helping you." Jun'ichi's gaze turned toward the floor, and his lips formed the slightest grin. "You say I am not vengeful, but you are wrong. I do not want to see Gennoveffa's plan through. We already have Hachirō. However, I want nothing more than to see Ayane's blood on my katana. Convince me that you won't die the moment you arrive at her doorstep.]"

Chapter 20

DAVID CLEARED A SPACE in the library's main hall. He began with the tables, piling loose books upon them first, and had Hachirō help him move each toward the walls. Then they gathered debris from a few shelves which had already collapsed in a corner near the stairs that led to the kitchenette. Finally, they pushed the shelves back toward the walls upon creaky old wheels—though a few were too rusty to move, or had already collapsed. The end result was an unevenly shaped oval of empty space—nothing but wooden floorboards and the dust in the air.

"Are you certain about this?" Hachirō asked after they finished.

Sweat had formed along the surgeon's brow. David could feel a dampness on his own back as well. No wonder people had stopped printing so many books—they were damned heavy.

"No," David answered. "I don't think I have a better choice, though."

Hachirō nodded. "I'll release him, then. If you're ready?"

David nodded, and the surgeon walked toward the storage room.

David had only a moment before he would return with Jun'ichi, and he still had no idea how he would beat the Tigre. He'd seen Jun'ichi fight. David kept thinking of that Heredes woman they chased down the prior morning and how quickly—how effortlessly—Jun'ichi dismembered her. Had she been wearing a dermal wrap, or any other kind of armor? David couldn't remember.

If Jun'ichi had a weakness, David didn't think that he would find it in Jun'ichi's mind, even shaken as he was by Gennoveffa's death. He was too disciplined for that. He wondered, however, if he could exploit a physical weakness. Jun'ichi had been chained up and starved himself for nearly twenty-four hours. Perhaps if David could keep the Tigre at bay for long enough, he would tire faster. That was also likely to tire David out as well. Aside from the fact he was probably twice the Tigres' age, he'd also been out of combat for a long time. Sure, he'd been in plenty of brawls with the cheaters and thieves that he and Maf tracked down, but most of them weren't fighters—just desperate. Jun'ichi would be a real challenge, the sort that David hadn't faced since the war. But, no other option came to mind.

David had found a piece of wood among the broken shelves that made for a decent bludgeon, the kind of stick that he used to play with as a boy when his family vacationed in the wilderness of Upstate New York. He'd always find a stick and hold onto it for the week, using it as both a makeshift walking stick and club—though he preferred to think of it as a sword back then. Swords were much cooler than clubs.

He pulled the club from the shelf it was still partially attached to and swung it around, testing the weight of it. If Jun'ichi came at him with his sword, it would sink into the partially rotting wood. He might even be able to overpower Jun'ichi with its weight. He had a hard time imagining the blade going through, no matter how sharp it might be. But how many times would that work? It had only taken one swing to remove the Heredes woman's hand. David had been trained in hand-to-hand combat as well as knife combat, but both were always meant to be last resorts. Most of his time had been spent training with pistols, rifles, and use of his mods. And he didn't want to use anything that might incapacitate Jun'ichi beyond what Hachirō's medi-gels could repair. When this was over, he'd still need the man's help with the Heredes.

David quietly cursed Jun'ichi for making him fight. They were wasting time and risking too much. And if David lost... He couldn't lose.

Jun'ichi reappeared with Hachirō. He prowled out of the hall like a predator, his eyes darting around the room—assessing it. A ring of blood remained around one of his wrists, though he'd picked most of the bullets out of his wrap. Jun'ichi's pistol and sword were both around his waist. David was suddenly quite glad that he lost the grenade launcher back at the water treatment facility. He wasn't sure that his wrap, or the library, for that matter, was built to withstand it.

After a moment, Jun'ichi locked eyes with David. He drew his pistol and flipped it over, pointing the grip toward Hachirō. The surgeon took the gun gingerly.

"[No guns. First to draw blood wins,]" Jun'ichi said.

As he finished, Jun'ichi drew his sword. It was about half the man's height, certainly longer than David's makeshift club. Even if he could overpower the blade, Jun'ichi would have a longer reach than him. David's wrap could probably deflect a few strikes, but it was already damaged from the car crash. He would have to be careful.

"First to draw blood," David agreed. "Don't chop anything off, though. I've had enough of my organics removed," he added, gesturing to his mechanical arm.

Jun'ichi did not respond.

David said, "If I win, you help free the Heredes' hostages."

"[When you lose, I will return Hachirō to the Tigres. Without you. We will deal with the Heredes how Mama Cinzia sees fit.]"

David loosened his tie and threw it off to the side. Was Jun'ichi trying to win the surgeon's bounty, or did he just want to hurt David? He steadied his grip on the club, transitioning to a Filipino grip, with his thumb up against the wood. He adjusted his feet to stand right foot forward, making his body a smaller target and giving his right arm better reach. His mechanical arm. It was unlikely that Jun'ichi's blade could break it, and making it bleed was out of the question. Jun'ichi must have realized the same thing, because he sneered back at David, but did not voice any objections. Instead, he raised his blade and charged forward.

Any plans that he had of overpowering Jun'ichi were immediately tested. It was all that David could do to dodge and block the barrage of slashes. Many found their mark and would have broken skin, had there been any on David's right arm. Jun'ichi moved at an inhuman speed. Something was making him faster—just enough to put David off-balance. He put out a signal with his remote and Jun'ichi's body became alight in bright green, yellow, and red pings on his HUD. Each represented something that he could connect with, though most of his mods were laden with firewalls or required hard wire access.

Jun'ichi took a step back, adjusted his grip on his sword, and walked around the room. David adjusted his grip on the club as well, holding it tightly, slightly concerned at all the notches that the Tigre's sword had left in it. Splinters arced out from the wounds at harsh angles.

David matched his opponent's movements, keeping some distance between them while he parsed all of the information on his HUD. Most of the mods on or in Jun'ichi's body were out of reach, but that helped narrow his focus down to the few that were. Most were fairly low-impact mods that, if interfered with, Jun'ichi would be slowed down at most. Others were cosmetic: David discovered that he could remotely change the color of the Tigre's light tattoo, but that didn't seem to be particularly helpful at the moment.

Jun'ichi lunged forward like an Olympic fencer, using his range to his advantage. He struck at David's shoulder, his legs, his torso, seemingly all at random. David tried to keep up, but his club was heavy and he couldn't predict where Jun'ichi's sword would go next. After a few seconds, his mechanical arm was straining to keep up. It didn't get tired the way a natural arm could—no lactic acid built up and no sweat formed—but it had a strict limit to how quickly it could move and react.

How long had they been fighting? A minute? Two? David had yet to achieve anything. He grit his teeth, trying to ignore the frustration churning in his chest. There was an answer to the Tigre's assault, there had to be. Otherwise he was going in solo against the Heredes, and Hachirō was going back to see Mama Cinzia early.

David charged the Tigre, swinging with his club. Jun'ichi dodged, hopped, and counterattacked. David felt the tip of his sword drag across his back. It tore his shirt nearly in half and scraped across his wrap.

Silence hung in the air. Footsteps echoed around the library as Hachirō walked around behind him. After a moment, he said, "[No blood.]"

David breathed a heavy sigh. Under normal circumstances, that attack would have cut through him—probably paralyzed him. He couldn't chance another charge like that, though. But simply defending himself wasn't a solution either.

Jun'ichi and David readied themselves again, as Hachirō retreated to a far corner of the room. David pulled his HUD back up. Red, yellow, and green lights flashed across his vision. He connected to a component that he'd spied earlier in Jun'ichi's cochlear implant: a small back-up battery. He uploaded a small package to it, an old script that he used to use in the military. It was almost certainly obsolete. That would either help him and make it harder to stop, since Jun'ichi's firewalls were designed for modern hacks, or it would make the script easily blockable. Either way, he sent it off through the Net—through their mutual connection to the public network. All he needed to do was keep the link active for a few seconds while the upload worked. A progress bar appeared on the periphery of his vision, quickly filling up.

David saw Jun'ichi's expression change, and a flash of red flitted across his eyes. An alert about the upload. David used the moment to strike at him, adopting Jun'ichi's stance and keeping his distance, but also refusing to let the Tigre focus on repelling the cyberattack. A fighter skilled with hacking could do both, but David suspected that Jun'ichi only operated in the Real. It had been Gennoveffa who dealt with La Ragna, after all, and she'd been the one to try and infiltrate the Heredes' network. At the time, David hadn't thought anything of it, but now...

He swung his club, batting away Jun'ichi's sword. It clattered on the floor. Finally. He went in for another attack, but Jun'ichi grabbed the club with one hand and struck with the other. David felt his fist connect with his chin before he saw it coming. Jun'ichi followed it up with a series of unarmed strikes across David's chest and arm. He stumbled backward, his back slamming against one of the bookshelves. It rattled against his weight. A book fell to the ground somewhere behind him.

"[What are you doing to me?]" Jun'ichi shouted, picking up his sword again.

So he hadn't blocked it. Good. All David needed to do now was outlast him. The progress bar was nearly full, grinding at eighty-five percent. David took up a defensive position as the Tigre swung his blade. Before, the sword had been a precision instrument. Every swing carried with it the years of practice and dedication. Now he moved like a butcher, swinging wildly, chopping, splintering the club until a fracture appeared down the middle of it. David tried to adjust so that he wasn't hitting the same spot, but it was too late, and the bludgeon snapped in half.

"[Answer me, bastard!]" Jun'ichi shouted, swinging, hair falling into his face.

David felt his wrap stop the blade when it collided with his side, but this time the Tigre did not stop to check for blood. His assault continued, blocked only by David's mechanical arm. His wrist finally caught the sword, and he closed the distance. Sparks and flakes of paint flew off of his arm as the blade scraped against it. Jun'ichi gripped David's head, shoving him away, and swung again. The blade scraped across his chest, where his wrap was thickest.

Two things happened at once. A pop echoed throughout the hall as the back-up battery in Jun'ichi's implant circuited. It caused a chain-reaction which damaged the main power source. Lights flickered across Jun'ichi's eyes, likely warnings and damage reports showing him what had happened. It wasn't just his cochlear implant, but all of his mods that relied on a connection to it or the RAM stored inside of it—they were all shutting down.

At the same time, David's mechanical arm split apart and the hidden blade within shot forward. He thrust with the knife, catching Jun'ichi's chest, right where a Heredes bullet had damaged his wrap. The tip pierced the armor and skin alike. He pulled his arm back just as quickly, the blade's tip a bright crimson.

Jun'ichi felt the wound, rubbing his bloody fingers together.

"[You won,]" he said, whispering to the ground.

David retracted the blade back into his arm. He said, "Let me help you—"

Jun'ichi raised his hand for David to stop. Still looking at the ground, he called out, "Hachirō. [Fix this.]"

The surgeon approached timidly. He shot David a glance, then put Jun'ichi's arm over his shoulder, and guided him back to one of the tables. David gathered Hachirō's surgical supplies and carried them over. When it was clear he wasn't needed, he went to the restroom to investigate his own wounds in the mirror.

Chapter 21

A drop of blood ran down David's side, between thin layers of near-invisible netting that made up the dermal wrap just above his skin. David stared at it in the bathroom mirror, a chill running up his spine and clawing toward his heart.

He found a package of toilet paper and dabbed at the spot until no more blood came. The seam between his skin and the wrap was still bloody, but at least it wasn't actively bleeding anymore. For now. The cut must have been shallow. He tucked the bloody paper into his pocket to make sure that nobody would find it in the trash.

The third closet that David found still had a few cleaning supplies left. They were old and musty, but the thin rag that he found toward the back was just what he needed. David wrapped it around his waist, over his sword-torn shirt. He looked like he was wearing a terrible Halloween costume of

Jack Danger, from the second act of *Search and Rescue* after the corpo's shadow board betrayed Jack and left him for dead. A few more good hits, and David suspected he would have also been left to die there on the library's creaky floor.

David took a deep breath, fixed his collar, and walked back to the main hall.

By the time he returned, Hachirō had already repaired the wound on Jun'ichi's chest. David hadn't cut very deep. However, the damage to the Tigre's cochlear implant was more severe. The overload had affected more than David expected. Jun'ichi couldn't hear out of his left ear, and his vision was blurry. His motor functions were impaired, since so many of them were enhanced by nanofibers that communicated with or through his cochlear. His legs, especially, seemed affected. They would sometimes spasm, often when Jun'ichi wasn't expecting it, and strain his muscles painfully. David tried to apologize, but the Tigre had no interest in hearing it.

When Hachirō needed help, or a tool from his bags, David did what was asked of him without comment. Otherwise, he spent a lot of time sitting around the hall, sometimes picking up a book to read. There were all kinds: memoirs about long-dead politicians and millionaires, cookbooks with faded pictures of dinners and desserts, and fictions about worlds with dragons and faeries. Those were his favorite as a kid, though he always preferred the movies. Still, he found a few old books to lose time in.

When they were beginning to get hungry, David left the library to pick up food. The surgeon had run out of curry. David put on his coat, making sure it hid all of his recent wounds and scratches, and left the library. Outside, it was nearly dusk. As he walked, he spied around the corners of intersections through a security or traffic camera, just to make sure nobody was lying in wait. He kept his time in the network short, careful not to attract too much attention.

David took an extra-long walk to a supermarket in Fiordini, a neighborhood just south of the library. It took forty minutes to get there, but if anyone was tracing his finances, it would at least throw them slightly off-track. He bought a package of water tablets, six containers of pad thai, and a few rolls. Enough for two meals. He also purchased a bandage and applied it in the market's bathroom, discarding his bloody paper and rag in the trash. The wound had started to bleed again sometime while he walked. The patch fit awkwardly over his damaged wrap, but it would at least help prevent it from bleeding onto anything. The bandage was also laced with medi-gel, so ideally it would help heal the skin. David wasn't sure how much of that would actually make it through his wrap, but for an extra three euros it was worth a try.

David made it back to the library without issue, though he was careful to check his corners and make sure nobody followed him, walking a different route that added another ten minutes to his travel. The sky was pitch-black as he returned to the library. When he entered the main hall again, Hachirō gasped in excited relief.

"You were gone so long, I thought you ran for the hills," he said.

"[I thought you were killed,]" Jun'ichi grumbled, staring off into the distance.

"Fortunately," David said, "neither. I just didn't want to buy anything too close to here. I got us some pad thai—"

"[Give it to me.]"

"And I picked up some bread," David finished.

"We should heat it first," Hachirō suggested.

"[I'll take mine now,]" Jun'ichi said, and reached out into the air. His eyes were unfocused, and he stared out at nothing in particular.

"I've still got some work to do," Hachirō explained. Then, to Jun'ichi, "[Are you sure? It will only take a minute to warm.]"

"[Somebody give me something to eat or I'll be bringing both your corpses back to Mama Cinzia.]"

"[Understood,]" Hachirō said.

David put a carton of pad thai into his outstretched hand. Before he could hand Jun'ichi any chopsticks, the Tigre had already torn the container open and began eating the noodles with his hands.

"[It is bland,]" Jun'ichi said.

David shrugged. "It's from an Italian supermarket."

"Ah," he said, and dug in for another bite. "[At least the garlic is fresh.]"

Chapter 22

After dinner, Hachirō went back to work repairing the damage to Jun'ichi's cochlear implant. He had the Tigre fixed within the hour, though he warned the repairs were somewhat fragile.

"[I was able to work around a few areas that were permanently damaged,]" he explained. "[However, that will put extra strain on the *working* parts. It won't break today or tomorrow, but you'll want to have it looked at as soon as we're done with the Heredes. I just don't have the equipment or parts here to repair it properly.]"

David had apologized to Jun'ichi a few times already at that point. He'd intended to disorient Jun'ichi during their fight, not cause any lasting damage. Each time, the Tigre shrugged it off without a word. So, as the night continued, David didn't bother to try and make amends. Instead, he focused on their next task. David shared the floor plans of the water treatment facility with Hachirō—Jun'ichi already had them—and they reviewed the maps together, planning out how they might get inside.

"[The front entrance was guarded when I arrived the other night,]" Jun'ichi said. Hachirō's electric lantern cast a sterile white glow over his snarling face. "[I did not see another way inside from the front, but Gennoveffa was able to get inside at some point. I didn't hear of any issues with her part of the plan—until things went wrong, of course. So, her hatch in the back must have worked.

"[However, the Heredes will probably have increased their watch. David suggested this earlier. But they were also optimistic about my defection from the Tigres. They are rebuilding the facility, and that makes them feel justified in whatever they do. The Heredes are overconfident, which we can use against them.]"

Hachirō nodded agreement. "I was happy to help them at first, for that reason. I'd rather the old place be working as well, but they intend to leverage control of it—and of course there's the kidnapping and murder. No telling what they'll do with it, or how they'll leverage the fresh water once they find a way to produce some."

"Of course," David said. He swirled a glass of water to help the purification tablet in it dissolve. "I'd rather go through the hatch in the back, here. The one Gennoveffa talked about using. You said it took some time for them to notice she was in—they might not even realize she went in that way. And if they've increased security in the front, it means there may be fewer people watching other angles. And there's a path along the treeline to the left, I don't think anyone used that last time."

Jun'ichi crossed his arms, staring into the lantern's light. He asked, "[David, how does that remote of yours work? How many targets can you hit at once?]"

"Just one at a time. And there's a lot of ways to block or intercept these signals. The Heredes' private network helps them in a lot of ways, but it's really hard to completely cut yourself off from the public network. Most of your gear was off-limits, either protected or off the Net, but not all of it."

"[How would you get access to the Heredes' network? For Gennoveffa, that was the key to getting Hachirō out.]"

David shrugged. "I'd probably have much easier access if we disabled it, or if I got access. But I would need to hard wire into something already connected to it. That would be the easiest, least noticeable way. Not that it wouldn't be noticeable—anybody actively using the network would catch us immediately. I could try with the remote, but that's even riskier. They wouldn't even need a diver to cut me off."

Jun'ichi produced a shard from the side of his head. He turned it over in the electric light.

"[What's that?]" Hachirō asked.

"[Gennoveffa planned to upload this into their network. She was convinced it would cripple the Heredes, but she needed a hard wire connection, and needed to maintain that link. You do not.]"

"What is it?"

Jun'ichi's eyes met David's. "[La Ragna's virus.]"

"[Wait, *the Spider?*]" Hachirō asked him, aghast.

"From the villa? They let you keep it?" David asked.

Jun'ichi frowned. "[No. Yet here it is.]"

"Do you mind?" David asked, reaching out. Jun'ichi placed it in his palm.

David slotted the shard in. He couldn't make out the specifics of how it worked, but it was clear just how complex the virus was. It attacked on multiple fronts, many of which were decoys, and would be a nightmare to remove once uploaded. Maf would have been able to understand it better, but all he needed to do was upload it to the Heredes' systems. The rest would—he hoped—work on its own. He focused on the lamp, the one electrical object that consistently worked in the library, and uploaded the code with his remote.

The library went dark.

David heard a clicking sound as somebody tried to turn the lamp back on. After a few uneventful moments, Hachirō said, "Well, I guess it works."

As dawn rose, David lay on the floor, using a stack of paperbacks for a pillow. He shut his eyes and jumped across the city, hopping between camera feeds and making his way north. He knew the route to the water treatment facility now, and made it there in about half the time as his last outing. The facility's cameras were all on the Heredes' private network, but he was able to use traffic and security cameras around the building to look around a bit. Nothing had changed since the prior day; the place was locked down, several guards posted at the entrance. He thought he saw a few more watching through windows, but it was hard to be sure. His vision was only as clear as the camera's, which wasn't saying much.

David snapped back to the Real. He blinked his eyes, casting away the sleep and tension from his sprint through the public network. He sat upright, careful not to disconnect the charging cable from his cochlear implant. His battery was still hovering around ninety-five percent. Still, his back ached fiercely. David did his best to stretch it even in his awkward sitting position.

He pulled the water treatment facility's floor plan up on his HUD, reviewing it for what must have been the hundredth time. La Ragna's virus was a massive boon to their rescue attempt, but David still hadn't found an access point that he liked. At this point, he wasn't sure that there were any good options. David kept trying the cameras and reviewing the floor plans anyway in hopes that something better than the hatch would reveal itself to him. After a few more minutes, he heard the others begin to wake. David gave up on finding a better way inside and disconnected the charging cable.

There was a little pad thai left over. Hachirō warmed it up for breakfast. Jun'ichi joined them in the main hall, and they ate in silence, seated around the broken lamp. Muffled sounds of traffic slipped in through the walls around them. The rice noodles seemed a bit off. Almost rubbery, perhaps.

David found a moment away from them in the kitchenette, where he filled a glass with water and tossed his last purification tablet into it. He listened to it hiss like a lit fuse as it dissolved. In the distance, he could hear Jun'ichi sharpening his sword with a whetstone.

Chapter 23

SHORTLY AFTER 12:00, DAVID picked up the pistol he took from the Tigres' armory and fit his extra clips into his pockets. Jun'ichi did the same. He looked like a wreck with his dermal wrap cracking, and his cochlear implant had clearly been messed with, but he carried himself with the same confidence as always.

Hachirō had left their van where he rammed into it the other night. Even if they had it, the vehicle would have attracted too much attention with all the broken glass and bullet holes. Hachirō drove them in the truck he'd hot-wired to escape the Heredes. He took them to a recharging station in Città del Nord, not far from the water treatment facility.

Before they left the truck, Hachirō gave David his contact in case they needed to change the pickup location, and wished them luck.

"I will stay close by, in case you need to get out quickly," Hachirō said. Then, to Jun'ichi he added, "[When my son is safe, I will answer to Mama Cinzia for what I took from her. So long as my boy is left alone.]"

Jun'ichi nodded at the surgeon. "[I will not bring Ichiro to her.]"

David didn't like the way he said that. Jun'ichi wouldn't bring Ichiro, but did that mean somebody else would? Was it in his power to decide that, even? Perhaps he was imagining things. David wasn't sure what anyone at the Tigres would want the boy for, though that hadn't stopped the Heredes. Either way, he couldn't help but worry what Mama Cinzia would do to make an example of the surgeon.

David left the truck, and Jun'ichi followed behind. They walked through an alley together, just as dark clouds rolled in, obscuring the sun. They made their way along a small footpath behind a row of shops, toward a thin treeline, where the ground was too steep for construction. David's feet slipped on the cold ground, and he used the trees to help balance himself as he made his way up the hill. Snowflakes fell, collecting on David and Jun'ichi's coats and their hair as they moved north. The air smelled of fresh snow—new and earthy. David cupped his hands over his mouth, the organic hand on the inside, and exhaled to warm it up.

A patch of trees surrounded the Heredes' facility. David led the way to a spot near the entrance, and stopped behind a few evergreens. He kneeled down beside them and signaled to Jun'ichi: *wait.*

The Tigre crouched next to him.

David took a deep breath. Nearby, a traffic camera scanned the road. He took command of it with his remote, closed his eyes, and the water treatment facility's front entrance came into view. Five Heredes were outside, their breath white and pulled apart by the breeze, all beneath a small awning. They were armed, but it seemed like at least a few were busy speaking with each other rather than standing at attention. That was good, but David couldn't get careless just because a few of them had.

He jumped to a different camera affixed below the roof of a nearby deli. It didn't have nearly as good a view, but it peered over a few other buildings and through a row of trees. Between the branches, he saw a Heredes standing watch in one of the facility's windows. He couldn't see well enough to tell if they were armed, but he had to assume they had a weapon on hand if not nearby.

He jumped to another camera, this one viewing the back of the building. The trees had been cut away there, making room for four pools through which the waters from Lago di Bolsena previously ran. Rusting pipes connected them into the back of the building. A woman crossed a small footbridge over them, then stopped near a hatch. She tapped against its side, and the doors spread open. She descended into the basement below.

David opened his eyes and motioned for Jun'ichi to follow him. He led the way to the back of the building, staying low, and careful about where he put his feet. It was all too easy to step on a branch or stumble over a rock hidden just beneath the snow. As they approached the back, their tree cover lessened, and he picked up his pace, dashing as quickly as he dared to the next patch of evergreens. He peered through them at the place where he saw the woman descend through the hatch. Nobody else was near, but there were cameras along the back wall.

Jun'ichi tapped the top of his wrist. *Hurry up*, David assumed.

David uploaded another of his old wartime codes to the camera: a glamor which made it look like they were just watching over a quiet snowy afternoon. Like placing a photo of the usual scene in front of it so that the camera didn't pick up what was actually happening in front of it. It was far easier to trick a person into seeing what they expected, rather than shut the cams off or hijack them. That would have raised suspicions the moment somebody noticed. However, it was difficult to focus on anything else while maintaining it. They needed to get inside and—ideally—disable the network. That would also draw attention, of course, but the Heredes wouldn't be able to pinpoint where the problem had come from at least. While they tried to reboot it, he and Jun'ichi could make their move.

Go, David motioned, and jogged to the hatch.

He inspected the side where the Heredes woman tapped it. The hatch was sealed with a biometric lock. David could have broken into it, but not while also maintaining the glamor, and they weren't completely out of the camera's view. He caught Jun'ichi's attention and motioned toward the lock silently.

Jun'ichi nodded and pointed two fingers toward his eyes, then away. *Keep watch.*

David drew his pistol while Jun'ichi worked on the lock. He hoped he wouldn't need to use it. The gun had no silencer, so the moment he needed to squeeze the trigger, the Heredes would hear come running. He held his breath while Jun'ichi worked, the Tigre's eyes alight as he connected a hard wire to the lock.

A few moments later, David heard a click, and the hatch opened. Jun'ichi disconnected and led the way down without a word. David followed him, catching his breath as he descended into the dark, shutting the hatch behind him. The lock clicked shut.

Chapter 24

DAVID SWITCHED HIS OPTICS to night vision, if only for a moment while he and Jun'ichi were in the darkest corner of the basement. The woman who walked through there earlier was nowhere to be seen. She probably left through a different door, because there were no lights on, and he heard no footsteps aside from a few coming from the floor above.

They were surrounded by supplies: mostly food, water, and purification tablets—enough to last the better part a year or more. More space had been cleared. It looked as though the Heredes were preparing for a siege.

Jun'ichi and David snaked their way through the basement, using the boxes as cover in case anyone happened to walk in. As they made their way into the facility, David's heart beat more quickly. He received an alert on his HUD and dismissed it. He tried to focus his breathing, rather than how dangerous this was, or wondering if they'd hurt Maf. His mind wandered back to the library, when Jun'ichi had called this a *suicide mission.*

David switched off his night vision as they reached an old wooden door illuminated by the light coming through a frosty hopper window. Through there, the Heredes' network was likely being maintained in a room two floors up, down the hall, and to the left—the facility's old control room, according to the floor plans that the Tigres got their hands on. Realistically, Ayane could have set up anywhere, but it would have been easiest where the old hard wire security system was built.

Jun'ichi raised a hand, counting down on his fingers: *three, two, one.*

He opened the door quickly, moving like a leaf on the wind. David followed the Tigre deeper into the facility, gently shutting the door behind him. They were in a spiral stairwell. It was the first time David had ever seen one outside of a horror movie, and it trembled under their feet, the old metal straining underfoot. Jun'ichi waved at him. *Quiet.* He continued up, easing his weight onto each foot slowly. David tried to mimic him as they scaled the strange old thing.

Jun'ichi stopped at the exit to the second story. When David took a position on the opposite side of the door frame, he put a hand on the knob and turned it slowly. He peeked through the crack as he opened it, paused, then shut it again.

David watched him closely.

Jun'ichi raised one finger. *One Heredes.*

He clarified in a message: *[13:10] One of Ayane's people, headed this way. I will take care of it, but be ready.*

"Marco?" a voice bled through the door. Footsteps approaching.

David drew his pistol and replied: *[13:10] If Ayane can't find him, how long before alarm bells go off?*

[13:11] This one's her driver, so it might not be long.

David grit his teeth.

"Marco, [stop playing games, I said I was sorry about—]"

The door opened. As the Heredes entered the stairwell, he locked eyes with David. A light flashed across his eyes, a question in his brow, and a shout bubbled up through his throat, but Jun'ichi had already wrapped an arm around his neck and dragged him into the shadows. David raised his pistol, wielding it by the barrel, and struck the man across the head with the grip.

It only took a second. When it was over, the Heredes man was limp. Jun'ichi watched David closely, and he thought back to when he pistol-whipped the Tigre, right before Hachirō T-boned them. Jun'ichi's furious glare suggested he was remembering the same thing.

David pushed the thought away and dabbed the spot where he hit Ayane's driver. He wasn't bleeding badly—it probably wouldn't even scar. He helped Jun'ichi tuck the man into the darkest corner of the stairwell. It would take a miracle for somebody passing through not to see him, but it was the best they could do for the moment. They would just have to hope that nobody came this way for a while—at least until they found Maf and Ichiro.

Jun'ichi checked the hall again. He stepped through this time, quietly making his way toward the control room. It was a small space, occupied by old computers and screens, an excess of analog keys and dials in front of them. Video of the facility and the outside of it displayed across some of the screens, while others remained black. They had been retrofitted with newer equipment. Wires not unlike those in La Ragna's lair ran along the walls, between the old monitors, and toward the center of the room. There, leaned back in a foldable chair, sat a Heredes diver. His headset was on, already inside the Net, body limp—fingers twitching slightly. A half-eaten apple, its golden skin nearly identical to the pale flesh, sat beside him on a desk. It hadn't begun to brown yet.

Jun'ichi began to draw his blade, but David put a hand on his and pushed it back into the scabbard. The Tigre glared at him.

"They will notice his absence. Keep an eye on the diver, but if we can leave him alone we should be able to stay hidden for longer."

"[If we leave him alone,]" Jun'ichi whispered back, "[he may become a problem later.]"

David shrugged. "I think he'll be too busy."

He stepped inside the control room and extended his hard wire, connecting it into an old port on the computer. Red text appeared across the center of his vision: *Unauthorized network. Are you sure you want to connect to HNn_02?*

He confirmed the link and began uploading the virus. A progress bar emerged on his periphery, ticking left to right. It would only take a few moments. Once the virus was uploaded, it would spread throughout the network, disabling it piece by piece. That would take a bit longer with the diver. If he noticed the virus—and if he was any good he would—he would probably delay its spread. But the way that the Tigres had spoken about La Ragna and having seen the virus work so quickly the other night, David wasn't concerned.

While that uploaded, David searched for Maf. It didn't take long. The Heredes had a camera watching her inside of a makeshift cell. The view wasn't very good, and the picture quality was lacking, but he caught a glimpse of her walking around the small room. Her black hair was pulled back, and her jacket no longer emitted any light. He didn't get a clear look at her face, but it was her.

David quelled the urge to tear the building apart and forced himself to take a closer look at where Maf was. It looked like some kind of storage closet, though it was mostly empty. David pulled up the floor plan on his HUD and turned to look at the wall so he could focus on reading the map. Based on that and the shape of it... Maf was probably on the ground floor, not far from the stairwell they'd come from. David would start there, then try the similar-looking rooms on the other side of the building. There was also a closet on the third floor which might have worked, but—no—that one had a window. David double-checked Maf's video, and couldn't see one, or the light of one. She seemed to be using a lamp similar to Hachirō's.

"Maf's on the ground floor," he told Jun'ichi. "We'll start with the storage room near the stairwell, then work around to the other side if she's not there."

"[What about the surgeon's child?]"

David checked the cameras again, flicking through them quickly. He saw Heredes, empty halls, snowy trees, and back to Maf's room—though she was out of view this time.

"I don't see him. We'll help Maf first, maybe she knows something. Hachirō suggested that the Heredes don't have much room, so they might have seen each other."

Jun'ichi shrugged.

It was a long shot, but David didn't want to delay getting Maf out just because they *might* find Hachirō's son. If they beat down too many doors, the Heredes would start coming after them. They might use Maf as leverage, more so than they already had. No, David wouldn't take that risk.

The progress bar on David's HUD reached completion, blinked at him, then slid away out of sight. As it did, the camera feeds blacked out, leaving behind only static and error codes. La Ragna's virus was in the Heredes' private network. David jacked out of the computer, letting the wire snap back into his arm.

David paused to look at the diver. His expression was mostly hidden by the headset, but he could see lines forming around it, the muscles in his neck tensing up and hands twitching. He was trying to fight the virus off.

Jun'ichi glared down at the diver, hand still on his sword. "[The other Heredes will notice this soon.]"

"Let's get back downstairs, then," David said.

He walked back toward the stairwell. Mercifully, the man they'd left unconscious was still unattended, and still unconscious. David hurried past him as quickly as he could manage without making too much noise.

David peered out from the stairwell once they reached the ground floor. It was wide open, for the most part. Low railings separated several walkways. In the center, pipes from the pools outside ran into a large and empty basin. Thin metal arms reached toward its center, their clamps empty—perhaps a place where filters used to go. A dozen Heredes stood around the far side of the basin. David recognized one as the woman who they followed inside. They were talking, relaxed. A few sat around a table playing cards, shouting and laughing with each other. It was good that they were distracted, but there were still so many.

Another group stood guard outside of the main entrance—the five they'd seen as they first approached the facility. They hadn't moved since they snuck inside.

One more Heredes guard stood alone outside of an unassuming door—the one that David suspected Maf was behind. Surely they were guarding *something*. An old combination lock had been fastened to the door as well. That would be tricky to break without being seen or heard. It was an analog lock, they'd need the combination or a key to open it, and there was nothing to hard wire into. One thing at a time, though. First, they had to deal with the guard, without getting caught.

David glanced at the machinery around the water basin in the center of the floor. He might be able to reactivate it remotely, but that would probably be too much of a distraction. They needed something that only the solo guard would go investigate, but this side of the floor was mostly empty.

Jun'ichi messaged him: *[13:23] The Spider*. Then he put a hand on the side of his head, tapping his cochlear implant, and mimed an explosion.

David grimaced at the idea. He didn't have a great sense of how quickly the virus would work. If it wasn't instant, the guard would alert the others. It would be easier if they could just distract her long enough to take her down like the man in the stairwell... But there was nothing else that David could think to do.

Jun'ichi repeated his hand movements.

David sighed, and scanned the lone guard's body for something he could target with the virus that would allow it to work instantaneously. There—a mod embedded with her brain, that would probably work. Some kind of neural augment. It had plenty of firewalls and protections against intrusions, but La Ragna's work had proved itself resilient to such things. It also seemed to have fewer firewalls than he'd expected—perhaps they'd been tied to the Heredes' network that the virus was actively tearing apart?

David sent the virus off. A few seconds later, red flitted across her eyes, and her body tensed up, like she was about to shout to the others. Then her eyes rolled into the back of her head and she collapsed.

David watched the Heredes across the basin, but they continued talking amongst themselves and playing their game. Nobody had noticed the woman collapse.

Jun'ichi put a hand on David's shoulder, and pushed past him. He walked casually, as if he belonged there. He pulled a thin metal rod from a container built into one of his wrists, an auto-key. They were illegal in most countries, since they could form to fit and pick just about any analog lock. He inserted it into the combination lock on the door, gave it a few turns, and it clicked open. It was stunningly easy.

David pushed through the door. Maf stood on the other side, bruised and bloodied, wielding a piece of a broken bowl. Her knuckles were white, the porcelain cut into the shape of a knife's blade. She dropped it as she locked eyes with David and it clattered to the ground, breaking in three pieces. She rushed toward him, throwing all of her weight into his. David wrapped his arms around her, nearly falling over, struggling to stay quiet. He kissed her forehead, dug his fingers into her hair, and breathed her in all at once. He needed to know that he'd found her, and he needed her to know the same.

Their embrace was cut short as Jun'ichi dragged the guard inside and shut the door. Drool touched the corner of the woman's mouth, and her arm was twitching.

"[My God,]" Maf whispered. Then, to Jun'ichi, "[What did you do to her?]"

He shrugged. "[It is your husband's doing.]"

Maf turned back to face him, a thousand questions on the tip of her tongue.

"It was Jun'ichi's idea. Don't worry, I'll explain later, right now we just need to get you out of here." He glanced at the porcelain. "Were you planning an escape?"

"I'd hoped to catch them by surprise, but I prefer your plan." Maf's expression hardened. She picked the submachine gun off the Heredes woman lying on the ground, checking its magazine quickly. "There was a boy here with me, but they took him away. David, he's Hachirō's *son*."

"Do you know where they took him?"

"I think so... They've been using an office on the other side of the building as a kind of negotiation or interrogation room. I don't know if he's still there or not, though."

Jun'ichi took a spare magazine and handed it to Maf. He said, "[You'll need this. Careful, those fire quickly. Don't want to run out of bullets.]"

"Right," she said, pocketing the spare mag. Her eyes lingered on the Tigre, drifting down to the fresh cracks and dents in his dermal wrap. "Jun'ichi. God. When they took me in that night, I saw Gennoveffa..."

Jun'ichi stared back at her.

"I'm so sorry."

He nodded, glancing down at the ground.

David put a hand on her shoulder. "There's not much time. Show us where Ichiro is, and—"

"Wait, how do you know his name?"

"We met his father."

"You met Hachirō!"

"Quiet, they may hear you. And yes, I'll explain that later, too."

"Right, fine. So we're *helping* Hachirō now, or?"

"[We came here to help both of you get out of here,]" Jun'ichi said. "[Now, can you take us to him?]"

"Okay, sure. Good. He's a good kid." Maf shook her head, seemingly bewildered. She toggled the safety off on her stolen weapon and took a deep breath. "Follow me. It's not far."

Chapter 25

A DECADE AGO, DAVID wouldn't have thought anything of their present situation. He'd been in worse scraps against more capable opponents, but after so long out of the force, having gone rogue the moment Hachirō enabled his mods, and seeing his wife wielding a submachine gun—it unsettled his stomach. They'd both been shot at, stabbed, and brawled more than once since they formed De Campo Investagatori Privati, but never on this scale.

But he had gotten her back. They were together again, and that was what mattered. And if he got a chance to tear the Heredes apart for kidnapping her, he gladly would.

Maf approached the door and opened it slowly. Through the narrow crack, David saw Heredes running toward them. David drew his pistol. Did they notice the guard was missing? Or perhaps they saw Jun'ichi dragging them into Maf's makeshift cell? Whatever the case, they would be ready for whatever came.

David was just about to put himself in front of Maf when he noticed that although the Heredes had run toward them, they all veered to the right—toward the stairwell. They were shouting to each other on their comms, calling out names, but of course La Ragna's virus had already disabled them. The virus hadn't spread to the rest of the Heredes' network, though. He'd thought by now that it would be affecting their mods as well. Had he misunderstood the way La Ragna's virus worked, or was the diver they left in the control room holding it at bay? Perhaps Jun'ichi had been right, and leaving him alive was a mistake.

"Hurry," David said. "Move to the left, keep low; we might get to the other side without them noticing. They're all focused on the stairwell."

"What's on the stairs?" Maf asked.

"Ayane's driver."

She rolled her eyes and pushed through the door. Before she even got a chance to peek around the corner, David heard a few Heredes shouting.

David stepped through the door. Two Heredes were walking in their direction, guns raised. David put a bullet in one. His heavy pistol kicked back, twisting his wrist. If it hadn't been made of reinforced metal alloys, he might have broken something. As he took aim at the second. They fired back, and bullets struck David's left side. He pulled the trigger and the second Heredes dropped. The man tried to get back up, and David fired twice more. They pierced the man's wrap and burrowed into his chest. His ears rang from the shots, but he could faintly hear more Heredes descending the rickety stairs. He took aim at the doorway.

"Run!" David shouted over his shoulder.

Maf and Jun'ichi sped past him. She ran toward the other side of the building, and the Tigre followed close behind. David quickly inspected his left arm and shoulder. His dermal wrap had protected him from the worst of it, but it was cracked on his shoulder. A piece of the wrap had nearly come off where one bullet struck him in the chest. It would still protect him from a blade or bludgeon, but the next bullet that hit him there would tear through his organics like nothing.

"David!" Maf shouted at him.

She was still running through the building, past the basin in the center. Jun'ichi had stopped near the main entrance, crouching low, pistol raised. He fired through the front doors at the guards posted there, who were running inside. Jun'ichi dropped three in quick succession, his railtech pistol piercing their wraps more easily. Two more were pushing through the attack as Jun'ichi's pistol clicked—out of ammo. He drew his blade and made to charge the remaining guards, but David was already pulling his trigger. The last two fell at the Tigre's feet, his sword left unbloodied. Jun'ichi paused a moment, then stabbed through the nearest Heredes' back anyway, glaring at David.

"Let's go!" David shouted at him.

They didn't have time for pettiness. Surely he'd have a chance to take out a few more as they made their way toward Ichiro.

Jun'ichi sheathed his sword and reloaded his pistol. He ran toward Maf, David keeping watch behind them. Maf kicked open a door ahead of them and fired her submachine gun into the hall. David couldn't see what happened, but she stopped firing. A haunted look glazed over her eyes, like she'd just woken up from a dream and realized what was happening—or perhaps she'd descended into a nightmare.

Shouting emerged from the other side of the floor. Half a dozen Heredes emerged from the stairwell he and Jun'ichi came from. Uesugi Ayane was among them, her hair tied back, a long sword in her hand.

"Tigres!" she shouted at them. "[You fucking cowards!]"

Jun'ichi stepped forward, but David stopped him. "Go with Maf," he told him.

"No!" Maf shouted at him.

David grit his teeth. They didn't have time to argue. Neither of them stood a chance against her unless David could find a way to upload La Ragna's virus to her. It was already in the Heredes' network, but the diver seemed to be keeping it from infecting anyone directly so far.

"Keep Maf safe," David told Jun'ichi. "You know I need to be the one to deal with Ayane."

"David," Maf pleaded with him.

Gunfire resonated around the walls, and she ran into the hall she'd cleared to avoid it.

Jun'ichi glared at Ayane, then David, and nodded. "[I agree,]" he said. "[But I must be the one to end her life. For Gennoveffa. Do not take this from me, David.]"

He nodded. David hadn't seen Ayane fight yet, but he had a sense that he couldn't pull his punches. If he gave her an opening, David suspected she'd run her blade through him as well.

Jun'ichi followed Maf down the long hall while David faced off against Ayane beside the empty water basin. He let the other Heredes run after Maf and Jun'ichi. They would be able to handle it. David needed to keep Ayane's attention focused on him.

Uesugi Ayane was taller than he remembered. It was the first time he'd seen her without her scarf and coat on, and she was built like a tank. Her body was more synthetic than not, with wires running above and under her skin. One patch of real skin on her arm bore her neon blue Heredes tattoo. He didn't recognize all of the mods she'd gotten installed, but he could tell that she would move fast like Jun'ichi and had thick armor on much of her body—not just a thin dermal wrap. It had been damaged recently, with ugly scars across her metal chest where somebody had tried to solder it back together. Had that been Jun'ichi's work, or was it an older wound?

David began uploading the virus to her, picking a mod that wasn't as highly protected as many of the others: a biomonitor under her skin, near her clavicle. The kind of device that most of her opponents probably wouldn't care about—but once La Ragna's virus was in her body, it would continue to spread. He just needed one domino to fall, and the biomonitor was an easy target.

"[I remember you from the villa. The American. What does your Tigre friend want now?]" Ayane asked, spitting the word *Tigre*.

"You killed his partner." David figured the longer he kept her talking, the better. He was relieved that she wanted to talk at all. As a flash of red danced over her eyes, David added, "A few nights ago, the woman who was here with him."

She seemed to blink away the warning, her attention fixed on David. "[The thief?]"

"All they wanted was Hachirō."

"[What in God's name makes that surgeon so important?]"

"He stole money from Mama Cinzia."

"[I would have given him back after we were done here!]" She raised her sword at David, but she stayed where she was. "[All this because *Mama Cinzia* wants to set an example. Exact a little vengeance.]" Ayane laughed dryly.

The upload was almost finished. The progress bar on David's HUD was near completion. Ayane hadn't noticed an alert about it yet, but she would soon.

"We might have come to negotiate if your people didn't shoot up that restaurant. We were in there discussing a peaceful solution when it happened."

Ayane grinned. "[A lucky tip from our mutual friend.]"

"What? Who?"

"[The Spider, of course. You stole something from them, too. I don't know what, but it pissed them off, so they asked us to help send a message. Seems you need to get new friends, American. They're all thieves.]"

Of course. Gennoveffa stole La Ragna's virus. The diver wouldn't want to leave something like that unpunished. What had they said when they met? A little reputation was a good thing. If people thought they could steal from La Ragna, that could spiral out of control...

The upload was at one hundred percent. A light flashed over Ayane's eyes. A system error message alerting her to a problem with her biomonitor. Would she notice what caused it, or just the malfunction? David raised his pistol toward her, uncertain of what would happen next. Moments passed like monuments, scraping by as lights continued to flicker across her eyes. Then her tattoo began to flicker. Another of Ayane's mods failing. She stared at it for a moment, then at David.

"[What did you do?]" she asked. Then again, raising her blade at him, "[What did you do?!]"

"That would be La Ragna's handiwork," he said.

Ayane lunged at him.

David dodged, hopped, and blocked her blade with his right arm. The sword left long scratches across the metal. He took a few shots at Ayane. Pieces of her armor scraped or chipped, but it was still mostly intact. She charged after him, stumbling over a lip on the ground. He backed up toward where they'd been keeping Maf and put a few more bullets in her. David was aiming for Ayane's head, but she was too fast. Even though she stumbled, even though she was fending off the spreading virus, he missed most of his shots on the second volley.

David tried to put more space between them but she was closing in, screaming, swinging her sword. At the last moment, David dropped his pistol. His mechanical arm split in two, and the hidden blade shot into place just as Ayane's sword neared David's chest. He caught her swing with it, the shimmering edge of her sword mere inches from his face.

Chapter 26

Jun'ichi put a hand on Mafalda's back and urged her forward. She resisted for a moment, but ran down the hall all the same. They leapt over a Heredes' body collapsed in their way—the one who Maf dropped moments ago—and paused at the end of the hall.

"Which way?" Jun'ichi asked her in Japanese.

Mafalda veered left. As they jogged, Jun'ichi almost missed the sound of footsteps coming from behind them. He put a hand out against her stomach and forced her to a stop.

"[I'm getting sick of you—]"

"Listen," Jun'ichi interrupted her.

He drew his pistol and aimed it down the hall where they'd come from. He nodded toward the hall, indicating that she should do the same. She raised her submachine gun and took aim as the footsteps grew louder. When the Heredes came around the corner, they opened fire, and two of the five dropped right away. Those in the back attempted to return fire, but they only succeeded in shattering a window behind Jun'ichi. He finished them off with a few well-placed shots.

Glass littered the floor, and a chilly winter breeze crept across the scene. Jun'ichi lowered his weapon, and Mafalda did the same.

"[That's all of them?]" She asked.

Jun'ichi walked toward the pile of bodies. He kicked their guns away, prodding the dead with his foot. When he was satisfied that they were in fact dead, he gave Maf a slight nod, and returned to her side.

"[Alright,]" she said.

Her voice sounded shaky. Jun'ichi remembered the look on her face after that first volley she fired down the hall, just before Ayane showed up again. It reminded him of Gennoveffa on the first job they'd done together, when she was new to the Tigres. She'd been a thief before, but never a killer. He'd ignored it then, and told himself it was none of his business. Then she'd hesitated the next time somebody pointed a gun at them. It nearly got them both killed.

Jun'ichi put a hand on Mafalda's shoulder.

She looked at it, then him, like he'd just said the strangest thing.

Jun'ichi said, "It is only natural to feel discomfort right now, but this is not the time. We all have demons. Keep going until the job is done. Stay alive, and you can wrestle with them later."

She nodded, and took a deep breath.

"[Thanks, Jun'ichi,]" she said, though the words sounded like a question.

He took his hand off her shoulder.

"Ichiro?" he reminded her.

"[Right. This way, I think he's in the old maintenance office. Last I knew, they were trying to figure out if he could pick up where his father left off. He told me that he can't. But he's worried they'll kill him, or something, if they find out.]"

She neared the end of the hall, where three doors led off in different directions.

"[The one on the left,]" Mafalda said.

Jun'ichi pushed his way in front of her and drew his pistol with one hand, the other on the doorknob. He paused a beat to let Mafalda fall into step with him, then twisted the knob and shouldered his way through.

There were three Heredes. A young man, unarmed and hunched over, sat between them. Jun'ichi shot one of the three Heredes in the head. A second charged him with a knife. Jun'ichi dropped his pistol and drew his sword, cutting across their chest. As they collapsed, their weight fell against

Jun'ichi's knees. As Jun'ichi stumbled backwards, the third Heredes took aim at him. He turned his back to them, where his dermal wrap was the least damaged.

A short burst of shots rang out, but he didn't feel any impact.

Jun'ichi looked around, and saw the final Heredes member leaning against the wall, eyes fading. He'd dropped his weapons and bullet holes lined his jacket. Blood spread around them, staining his shirt.

Mafalda stepped forward, her submachine gun in hand. She asked, her voice shaking slightly, "[Ichiro, are you okay?]"

The boy was older than Jun'ichi expected, maybe eighteen. His skin was a shade lighter, but Ichiro otherwise looked like his father, down to the long black hair and short beard.

"Maf!" Ichiro exclaimed, then staring at Jun'ichi, he said in Italian, "[Who is he?]"

"[A friend. Hurry up, we don't have long. Take this.]" She took a pistol from one of the fallen Heredes and put it in his hand.

"[I don't know how—]"

"[Point and pull the trigger. But only if you have to.]"

"[Do I need to turn on—]"

"[Just don't aim unless you intend to use it, and careful who you point it at.]"

Ichiro nodded, his face pale and sickly-looking.

"[Okay, but…]"

Ichiro was holding his leg. Blood dripped down it.

"[Shit,]" Maf said, and took a look. "[Keep pressure on it. It doesn't seem too bad, but we need to get out of here. Lean on me, I'll help you outside.]"

Jun'ichi checked the door. The way was still clear for the time being. He couldn't hear anyone coming, either. Most of the Heredes were probably already dead—there hadn't been that many to begin with. But Ayane was still fighting. Jun'ichi could hear her yelling and crossing blades with David in the distance.

"I need to go back," he said. "I cannot let David finish this fight without me."

"[Back where?]" Ichiro asked.

"[My husband's by the main entrance keeping Ayane off our backs.]"

"[She'll kill him,]" Ichiro said, his eyes wide.

"She will do no such thing," Jun'ichi told the boy. "David has been dismantling her systems all this time. The longer she fights, the more her mods will break down. And I will end her before she can harm another soul. But I must return if I am to finish the job. Will you two be okay?"

Mafalda put Ichiro's arm over her shoulders and helped him up. "[Go, we're right behind you.]"

"Thank you," Jun'ichi said, and ran back toward the center of the facility. He could hear Mafalda and Ichiro speaking behind him. A part of him wanted to hang back and make sure they were safe, make sure they were staying close, but she still had her submachine gun—and he desperately wanted to run his blade through Ayane's ruinous heart.

Chapter 27

David thrust his blade at Ayane's chest. La Ragna's virus had made her movements sluggish and clumsy, but she was holding her own. Her sword had already drawn blood from David's left shoulder and right leg, and a swift kick he took in the side had probably broken a rib or two. He hadn't gotten a chance to inspect it. Ayane's assault was relentless, but she was beginning to show signs of fatigue. She swung her blade a bit too wide, and she was slow to recover. David took advantage of her slow recovery and lunged forward with his dagger. It pierced her armor where two pieces had been soldered together. It didn't go in deep, but when he yanked the blade free it came back tipped in crimson.

Ayane swung her sword wildly, the edge biting into David's chest, tearing his shirt and skirting across the thickest part of his wrap.

"[You're ruining everything,]" she screamed, red lights flickering across her eyes. In the time they'd been fighting, her mods had continued to fail. As the virus spread, David uploaded it to other parts of her body. The last upload to a heat sink in her back had nearly cost his head.

David leaned back as she swung again, her sword tearing at his shirt's collar. He took another step back, wheezing, hardly able to catch his breath.

"[We drink poison every day.]" She yelled at him between attacks. "[And the corpos sell us the cure.]" Another swing—this time David caught it with his blade. She glared at him, a fire in her eyes—the kind that threatened to burn both David and herself. "[This place could have helped push us in the right direction. It could have been the start of a real revolution.]"

David held her gaze. "You kidnapped people to make it happen. You hurt my wife."

She raised her sword and swung again.

David caught it with his blade again.

"[You helped the Tigres attack us,]" she said.

Ayane was visibly having trouble moving. Was this argument a stalling tactic? David feinted an attack, then reached an arm around her neck. Ayane twisted her body around before he got a chance. He barely had time to defend with his mechanical arm, which was already littered with scratches and shallow cuts.

"The Tigres weren't even interested in you until you refused to give up the surgeon."

"[You're just a merc.]"

"Now you're just calling me names."

Ayane screamed and swung at him. David caught the blade, then redirected it under his mechanical arm. He trapped it against his side, and thrust his blade into her wrist. Ayane shouted and took a step back, letting go of her sword. She pressed against where his weapon had pierced her wrist.

David retracted his hidden blade and took up Ayane's sword instead, leveling it at her. David breathed deeply, his chest heaving, sweat dripping down his nose. He'd actually beaten her.

"Put your hands on your head," he said.

"[What are you, police?]"

"I'm trying to end this before more people lose their lives. I'm trying to protect you."

She laughed. "[How very *American* of you, pointing a weapon at a woman and telling her you're *protecting* her. You're not in control. Even with your stolen viruses and military tech. You never were.]"

Ayane reached out to either side, grinning madly, and the metal around her arms shifted. Panels parted, wires exposed, and blood dripped down her fingers. Long blades emerged from her arms. They folded forward like a pair of scythes, though the right one failed to extend quite as far as the left. It was little comfort as Ayane charged him, reaching out with her shattered hands and long blades like a praying mantis.

David raised Ayane's sword to block the attack, but before she could make contact, somebody rammed into her. She crashed into a wall. Jun'ichi stood in her place, taking aim at her with his pistol.

"[Go help Mafalda. I will finish this,]" he said.

"Where is she? Ichiro?"

"David!" Maf called to him. She was just coming from the hall. A young man leaned against her for support. He held a pistol in one hand, and pressed his bloody leg with the other. "Ichiro's hurt, we've got to get him out of here, now."

"Fuck. Okay, Jun'ichi, can you handle this for a minute?" David asked him.

Ayane, just getting up, eyed them like a feral animal, her long blades scraping against the floor. The metal in her arms shifted again, and the long blades split into four, each. End one moved independently, like long razor-sharp fingernails.

Jun'ichi adjusted his stance and took a deep breath. "[I've been looking forward to this,]" he whispered.

"I'll come back as soon as I can," David told Jun'ichi.

Jun'ichi raised his pistol and fired it until the clip ran dry. Ayane stumbled under the armor-piercing shots, which seemed to have cracked the scaly plates across her body. Still, she stood back up uneasily.

Jun'ichi drew his sword. "[This ends now.]"

David ran back to Maf and helped to support the boy's weight. "What happened?" he asked.

"He got shot," Maf said.

"How bad?"

"It could have been much worse, but it's not great, either. It needs to be seen."

"Alright, let's get him outside."

As he spoke, David sent Hachirō a message: *[13:44] Ichiro is hurt. Meet us in front of the Heredes' facility. He needs to get away from here. The front guards are gone.*

Just behind them, Jun'ichi fought wordlessly with Ayane. Their blades were a blur as he pushed her back toward the empty basin, keeping her away from them. Even so, as they approached the exit, David kept an eye on her, wary of how easily she seemed to overcome La Ragna's virus. The woman before had crumpled after a few seconds. He struggled to understand how she was still standing.

They stepped over the bodies of Ayane's guard who once stood watch over the main entrance. When one of them moved, Maf let a few bullets loose into his back without breaking her stride. David looked at her over Ichiro's head. She kept her eyes forward.

Hachirō responded: *[13:45] I'm almost there. How bad is it? [13:45] Doesn't seem too bad, but he's having trouble walking.*

As David sent the last message, he saw Hachirō's truck emerge through the entrance. He swerved around most of the Heredes' parked cars, and scraped past or rammed through those he could not. He came to a stop a few feet from David, Maf, and Ichiro.

"[Father,]" Ichiro said in Japanese, breathing heavily.

David looked down. The walk had made his wound bleed more. Some had gotten on David's pants.

"[Ichiro!]" Hachirō said, opening his door.

"Stay inside!" David told him, and forced it shut. "I don't want you catching a stray bullet. Could still be a few Heredes walking around. Maf, help me get Ichiro into the passenger seat."

Hachirō watched anxiously as they walked around the front of the truck. By the time they got to the other side, Hachirō was rifling through the back, looking for something.

"Careful of your leg," Maf told the boy as they helped lift him up into the high seat.

To his credit, Ichiro barely made a sound. Blood ran down his leg and onto their hands and the seat. He winced and clung to their hands, the door, then the truck's grab handle.

His knuckles were white and his breathing was heavy. He was probably in shock.

Hachirō emerged from the back with a blue rod and a towel. He snapped the rod and a light on one end of it illuminated the cabin a light blue. "[Wrap this in the towel and keep it on the wound, it will keep everything cold and help reduce bleeding. I'll take a proper look when I can.]"

"You have a place you can go to do that?" David asked them.

"The library."

"No, Jun'ichi knows where that is."

Hachirō stared back at him, confused.

"Do you have a place outside of town?" David asked. "Or, better yet, out of the country."

Hachirō thought for a moment. "I know a woman in—"

"Don't tell us. Just go."

"I told Jun—"

"I know. But Ichiro needs your help. He needs you. I think Jun'ichi might have warmed up to you, in his own way, but Mama Cinzia will want to make an example of you. That's why she contracted us. You stole from her and now you've indirectly gotten one of her people killed. So I'm telling you to get out of here."

"David," Maf said, and put a hand on his shoulder.

"What will Mama Cinzia do to Hachirō if he goes to her, Maf? What will Ichiro do afterward? I don't like it. I'm fucking sick of the Tigres and the Heredes. Both of them. We started our business to help people, not do their dirty work. The deeper we get with them, the more we become part of this... This mutual need for revenge, whether it's for theft or violence. One hurts the other, who punches back harder, and so on. That's how you get shit like the Rivos. The animosity just builds, and I'm done with it."

Her expression hardened. "She will come for us."

Hachirō said, "I don't want to cause trouble."

"No," Maf said. "She will not work with us again. She may come for us. We need to be prepared for that. You, however, will be long gone."

David pulled her close. "Grazie." Then, to Hachirō, "Get some new wheels somewhere. Jun'ichi saw this when you drove us here, they will be able to pull up his memories to track it down. Trade it in as soon as you can, ideally with somebody who won't record what you took off the lot."

"And that wound doesn't seem too deep," Maf added, "but it could cause problems if you leave it too long. Pull over somewhere quiet and wrap it up. You have supplies for that?"

"I have enough," Hachirō said, his eyes wet.

The building's front doors swung open, their glass windows shattering as Ayane fell through them. She collapsed on the ground, rolling through the snow. Two of the blades on her right hand were broken in half, and those on the left were slick with blood. Jun'ichi stepped forward with a limp, then paused, eyes locked on Hachirō's truck.

"Go!" David told Hachirō.

Maf slammed Ichiro's door shut. Jun'ichi yelled at them as Hachirō put the truck in reverse. Mud and snow sprayed as he turned then sped out onto the road. David listened to his engine fade away as he sped off.

"There goes the contract," Maf said, longingly.

"Good thing that family from Calanchi gave us a tip." David watched Ayane stand back up, her movements shaky, her armor fractured, and a red rage in her eyes. "She's still fighting. Goddamn."

"She looks like [death,]" Maf muttered.

David took a step forward and raised Ayane's sword, tightening his grip on it. Maf took up a spot next to him and checked her submachine gun's magazine.

"Not many shots left in this one, and only one more mag left."

"Make 'em count," David told her, "and be careful."

Behind Ayane, Jun'ichi moved forward, though David could tell he was looking past her—at him. For a moment he thought the Tigre was about to attack them for letting Hachirō go. David wasn't sure they could hold them both off. Both Ayane and Jun'ichi were better with a sword than he was, and Maf was low on ammo. He'd dropped his pistol somewhere in the old facility.

David held out a hand toward Jun'ichi, a tightness growing in his chest. Sirens sang in the distance. Were the police in Montefiascone also controlled by the Tigres? They'd certainly had some influence over those in Zepponami at the start of the job.

Before David got a chance to try and convince Jun'ichi to work with them, Ayane laughed. "[I will see you fall,]" she growled. The bloodlust faded from her voice. She sounded tired, and spoke with such certainty that she could have been relaying the current weather or today's stocks. "[I will see you all fall,]" she said.

She took up a defensive pose, facing David and Maf, eyes alight. A spike of energy registered on David's HUD, and a collage of signals overlaid on top of her mods turned red. Shockwaves of energy pulsed through her body even as La Ragna's virus took hold. She wasn't fighting it anymore. Her attention seemed to be elsewhere—then it struck him. She was overloading her mods, just as the first Heredes had when they ran her off the road, trading her life for a burst of speed and strength. She'd only had a few mods, though, and Gennoveffa had been there to help. Now...

"Shoot her," he shouted at Maf.

As she fired, David ran forward. They had to stop this before she powered up any further.

Bullets glanced off and picked away at Ayane's armor. She screamed into the afternoon sun, and dashed toward David. She was a blur, practically disappearing and reappearing wherever she desired. David raised his sword to block her blades just in time, the force from her strike shaking his grip. Ayane pulled back, jumped to the side, and swung again. David blocked one hand, and she stabbed at him with the other. Broken blades pierced his side, one finger through the crack that Jun'ichi had made during their duel. David grunted, gritting his teeth. Ayane smiled a bloody smile at him, red lights obscuring her pupils.

Sirens hung in the air, ever closer. A new volley of rounds slammed against Ayane's shoulder and head. She turned to face Maf and pulled the broken blade from David's side. She took a step toward her, but Jun'ichi grabbed Ayane's ankle. He dragged her backwards and set her off-balance so she was unable to make use of her extreme speed. David took advantage of the moment and slashed across her stomach, but the blade glanced off her tattered armor.

Ayane turned and swung at Jun'ichi. He raised his blade to block her. David's HUD indicated a rising temperature in Ayane's chest—something inside of her was overheating.

"Don't let up!" David shouted.

Jun'ichi grimaced at Ayane, but he kept pace with her attacks, and even got a few of his own in, but nothing that drew blood. David tried to help, taking a few swings of his own, but his shattered wrap was making it hard to move. Every step and swing sent a shock of pain through his body. Or was that his possibly-broken ribs?

Another rattle of shots echoed. Bullets struck Ayane in the back and she stumbled. She caught herself quickly, then spun back and stomped toward Mafalda. David stood in her way, slowing her down, but he was so much slower than her. He blocked one, two strikes, but a third landed on his shoulder and sent new cracks through his wrap. The blade's edge bit into his skin, drawing blood.

David grabbed Ayane's arm and drove her sword into it. The blade didn't pierce her arm completely, but it jammed into something, and a line of blood formed where he'd struck her.

Ayane pulled back her arm with the broken blades, primed to strike him with it, when the tip of a sword emerged through her chest. Her muscles relaxed as she stared down at it, her jaw slack. Behind her, Jun'ichi shouted, and the blade went deeper—the tip emerging like a long horn between her lungs. Then, a loud *crack*. Ayane gasped, and the lights faded from her eyes. She looked up at David, lips slightly parted, as if she wanted to tell him something. They moved wordlessly, quickly. Then Ayane collapsed as Jun'ichi threw her body to the ground. She landed face down in the mud and snow. David could see the dozens of cuts, indentations where bullets had damaged her armor, and finally the large gash where Jun'ichi's blade finally ripped through her armor and mods. Half of the sword remained inside of her. Sparks illuminated the bloody wound, and one of Ayane's legs twitched.

David looked away from the carnage.

Jun'ichi stood in front of him, one hand pressed against his bleeding leg, the other still holding his sword. The broken blade had snapped inside Ayane. The Tigre stared at the shattered edge, turning it over in the light, staring as if under a trance—or perhaps as if one had lifted. He frowned at it and whispered, "[Be at rest, Gennoveffa.]"

Chapter 28

IN THE WEEKS FOLLOWING the death of Uesugi Ayane, David and Maf were questioned by multiple detectives, and a police car was often parked across the street from their home office. No doubt some of them were relaying information back to Mama Cinzia. The Tigres' boss hadn't requested to meet with them, nor did they care to seek her out, but Maf insisted that she was watching them.

After the police removed the dead from the old water treatment facility, somebody new moved in. They were under a different name—*Soluzioni Italiane*—but DAvid and Maf were convinced that the corp was funded and staffed by Mama Cinzia. Soluzioni Italiane announced at a press conference that they were investigating whether or not the old plant could be revitalized, promising to rebuild if it could not be. Their spokesperson went on RAI 3 speaking idealistic platitudes about the need for local sources of fresh drinking water, condemning the events at the plant, but celebrating the attention that it brought the issue.

Behind the new company's spokesperson stood a familiar figure. Jun'ichi was dressed in a tight-fitting suit, and he'd gotten his hair cut short, but it was undoubtedly him. What role he had in the revitalization of the plant, David had no idea. In an ideal world, he would never find out. Still, he was happy for the Tigre. He wasn't a bad person, just a bit grim, and fiercely protective of his own. If he could channel that into helping provide people fresh water... Perhaps there was hope yet. David wasn't about to hold his breath, though. He worried that they'd simply traded one threat for another.

David turned the feed off, and RAI 3 blinked away from his HUD. The sound of the broadcast was replaced by the sizzling of tuna in his frying pan. He spiced the burgers with salt, chicory, and chili powder and put them on buns already prepared with tomato slices. Juices dripped down into the bread as he topped it.

David put a plate in front of Maf, who was seated at the kitchen table, her gaze locked on the street through their window. The police car which usually watched them was missing that afternoon. Still, her thoughts were elsewhere, her movements slow. Her fingers touched the edge of the plate, but she didn't acknowledge it or David otherwise.

David sat beside Maf, wrapping an arm around her. He kissed her shoulder and asked, "Where are you?"

Her hand reached out and wrapped around his. "Here," she answered. Her fingers were ice cold.

"Try again."

She squeezed his hand. "I keep thinking that they'll want something more from us. Or for us to pay off Hachirō's debt. I don't know. It's hard to imagine that after everything that happened... It's suddenly just *over*."

"If they wanted something from us I think they would have said or done something by now. Or they wouldn't have paid us for the job." He rubbed her shoulder. "But if you want I can reach out."

"No," she said, a smile on the corner of her lips. It faded just as quickly. "I just don't feel safe here anymore. We've always known the Tigres were everywhere here. This wasn't even the first time that we worked with them, so it feels ridiculous but—"

"Non è ridicolo," David interrupted her.

He took her by the chin and gently turned her head to look up at him. Tears welled in the corners of Maf's eyes. David pressed his lips to hers, lingering in the moment, breathing her in. She touched his chest, and he felt it.

They'd both been scarred by their fight with the Heredes, but he'd taken the brunt of the hits. The clinic they visited stitched Maf up, but had to remove David's dermal wrap. It was too badly damaged to be repaired. He was due to go back in a week to have a new one put on, but he'd found that he liked having it off. He'd worn one for so long that he'd forgotten the subtle ways that a wrap could limit him. The weight of it was gone as well as the armored chest piece attached to it. Even little things like feeling the breeze against his skin or Maf's touch felt different without it.

Maf had signed up to get a new wrap as well, the same kind he'd ordered. It wasn't quite military-grade, but it was as close to one as a civilian could get. He'd thought she was simply being pragmatic. A wrap was insurance against dangerous jobs they might take in the future, but now...

David opened his mouth to speak, but somebody knocked at the door. Their heads snapped to the moving shape. David's heart slowed when he noticed the man get back into his van: a white vehicle with *Poste Italiane* written on the side.

He opened the door and took the small package inside.

"Who is it from?" Maf asked.

"No return address."

Maf made a face.

"I'll open it here," David said, and took a step away from her.

"Hold it away from your face. And use the robot arm to grab whatever's in there."

"Right," David said.

He tore open the package, angling it away from himself. No powder fell out of it, nor any creatures, and nothing exploded. A fantastic start, so far. David looked inside and saw the spine of a book. It was eggshell white, with faded text along it.

"Did you order a book?" he asked.

"Like, a real one? No."

David pulled the book from the packaging. It was old, made entirely of paper, worn and wrinkled from age. The cover was plain, with thin black letters across the top made to look as though they'd been painted on: *Ikigai*.

David couldn't help but smile at it.

"What is it?" Maf asked.

He showed her the cover.

"That doesn't explain anything," she said.

"It's from Hachirō. He and his son made it, wherever they were going."

"How do you know?"

"Hachirō showed me this book when we were hiding in that library I told you about. He sent this to tell us he was alright, I'm sure of it."

David flipped quickly through the pages, then set the book aside. Maf still hadn't eaten a bite. Although to be fair, he hadn't either.

"I forgot water," David said, and quickly grabbed two glasses.

He was in the middle of filling one when Maf suggested that he get a bottle of wine instead. He set the glasses down and picked a Tuscan rosato. As he was pouring it, he noticed that the water he'd poured before was clearer than usual. He paused just long enough to swirl it in the glass. There were still contaminants, but it wasn't as bad as usual.

David brought the rosatos over to Maf and sat back down with her.

"What if we left the city?" he asked.

Maf smiled at him. "What do you mean?"

"I mean, I don't know how much longer I can keep up this pace. Crawling around in tunnels and fighting criminals... Plus, I like the feeling of *not* having a dermal wrap all over my body. Hachirō can get out, why not us?"

"Where do you want to go?" she laughed.

David shrugged. "I've never been to Greece. And you know I love their music."

"It's no better than Italian music."

David shrugged.

"[It's no better than Italian music,]" she said more forcefully, her smile betraying the severe tone.

"Or I could take you to the States," he pivoted. "I've shown you the city, but there are so many other places. My family used to vacation in the Catskills. They still have the old ski lodge at Hunter Mountain. And if you show up a bit early, the autumn colors are like nothing you've seen here."

Maf laughed. "Stop it."

"No, I'm serious."

Maf wrinkled her brow at him. "David, we have a life here. We have a business. What would we do in Greece or New York?"

"Between the last couple jobs, we have a cushion. Won't need to figure out what's next for a minute. But I'm sure we'll come up with something. Maybe you can do something with coding—you made a whole trojan in a few hours, remember. And every town needs a beat cop. Maybe we'll find a quiet place, somewhere where the most dramatic problem is a cow standing in traffic."

"You're being ridiculous."

"There are loads of towns like that."

"Okay."

"I'm serious, Maf. Let's get out of here. You just said yourself that you don't feel safe here. I'm ready for a change too. Let's go figure it out together." He raised his glass. "What do you say?"

She eyed him carefully, weighing his words. Then, she clinked her glass against his, and said, "[Alright.] Let's go and see your cow towns, David."

Acknowledgements

Firstly, I'd like to thank *you* for reading *Animus Paradox!* I hope you've enjoyed spending a little time in the world of Digital Extremities with David and Maf. If you have time, please consider writing a review! They're a massive help.

Thanks to my editors Bard & Butter, and especially B.K. Bass, who originally put the idea for this story in my head as he and I edited my prior short story collection *Digital Extremities*. Additional thanks to Andy Peloquin, Nina Voss, A.J. Calvin, Paul G. Zareith, and everyone else who read and reviewed the book early. Your enthusiasm and encouragement has been nothing short of incredible.

I'd also like to thank my cover artist Ahmed Elgharabawy (@redpharaohart), who took my indecisive ramblings and turned them into something fantastic.

About the Author

Adam Bassett is an author, designer, and illustrator originally from Northern New York. He is the author of *Digital Extremities* and *Animus Paradox*. He has also previously appeared in anthologies such as *Blooms of Dawn* (SmashBear Publishing) and *Nature Erupts* (Two Doctors Media) and previously volunteered as the editor-in-chief at Worldbuilding Magazine.

Visit adamcbassett.com to see more of his work and subscribe to his newsletter for updates about what may come next. Or, follow him @adamcbassett on Bluesky, Instagram, or Threads.

Content Warnings

Animus Paradox contains descriptions of surgery, kidnapping, violence, gore, and death. It also contains (mostly) off-page references to organized crime and terrorism.